D0804737

SARA GALLARDO

LAND OF SMOKE

Translated from the Spanish
by Jessica Sequeira

PUSHKIN PRESS

LONDON

Pushkin Press
71–75 Shelton Street
London, WC2H 9JQ

Copyright © The Heirs of Sara Gallardo 2018
English translation © Jessica Sequeira 2018

Land of Smoke was first published as
El país del humo in Argentina, 1977

First published by Pushkin Press in 2018

1 3 5 7 9 8 6 4 2

ISBN 13: 978 1 78227 403 2

All rights reserved. No part of this publication may be
reproduced, stored in a retrieval system or transmitted
in any form or by any means, electronic, mechanical,
photocopying, recording or otherwise, without prior
permission in writing from Pushkin Press

Frontispiece: Sara Gallardo, first printed in *Confirmado*

Designed and typeset by Tetragon, London

Proudly printed and bound in Great Britain by
TJ International, Padstow, Cornwall

www.pushkinpress.com

To H.A. Murena

CONTENTS

LAND OF SMOKE

ON THE MOUNTAIN

THINGS HAVE CHANGED NOW. In those years, life wasn't enough for us to finish off the Spaniards.

I once met a grenadier whose foot teemed with maggots; he pulled them out with a tiny stick. He'd say 'Another one, go die,' day in and day out. If you look at it the right way, all of us were just like him. Day in and day out the same obsession: to finish off the Spanish in America. They were the maggots that fed on liberty, and vice versa. We were the maggots eating away the empire, without mercy.

I was left for dead in a terrible place, the Andean *cordillera*. Very high up, some mountain range in Peru.

I'm from the pampa. The crags, the wind, the condors big as I am, the paper sky... I'm terrified of the mountain. With the regiment I could bear it. But when I opened my eyes in the silence, and found myself alone...

The condor landed on the rock and fixed its round eye on me.

'If I stop looking, it will start,' the idea came to me. What would start? What I'd seen so many times before: eyes gouged out, the fluttering, the greedy naked necks sinking, emerging bathed in green stuff. Amidst the feathers, the corpse seemed to move.

'If I stop looking…' And I did stop, for who knows how long. I had my wounds to keep me busy.

The sun, too. At that height you can't imagine what the sun is like. The shadow either. Look for shelter and you find ice, look for warmth and you step in a bonfire. And so you die in two different ways, and the mountain stays indifferent.

Without the *cordillera*, without condors, without sun, without shade, I'd still have had the wounds: my broken leg, my broken arm, my broken ribs, something on the side of my face.

And the thirst. The thirst was worse than all the rest put together.

Around me were snowy peaks, hunks of raw flesh and pampas the colour of gold, false as death.

Why was I alone? A horseshoe near my foot and a cannon were my company. Not a corpse, a voice or a gun in sight. And the condor waiting.

I thought: I'm dead. The pain proved me wrong.

I came to understand that I'd fallen off a cliff, no doubt the mule's fault. We'd always hated each other. It probably fell out of pure spite, dragging me and pieces of stone along, the cannon falling off its back along the way. It was certain it had gone on falling a long way – the horseshoe was its farewell letter – and a flurry of activity by the condors suggested it was lying further down. If I could have felt joy, I would have.

I suppose those condors served as a signal.

When I opened my eyes the light had changed. A gag choked me, my tongue. A mushroom slid past, or a turtle (I started to think I was dead again). No, it was a human figure under a leather hide, furtive, hunched over, armed. He fought the condors for what was left of the mule.

I said, 'For the love of God…'

No voice came from me.

I yelled, 'Brother, for the love of God.'

My next memory is darkness. I'm no longer thirsty, and am bound like a salami. A little noise: *chac chac*. My tinderbox. A small flame leaps up. I see a being, a gleam of bald forehead. Crouching, he starts a fire. Flames rise. Leaning over the flame, he sobs.

Daytime. The place turns out to be a cave. I'm still bound, for medicinal purposes, with furry strips of hide. Rocks close off the entrance. At certain times, I hear them moving; close my eyes, peer. The being wrapped in pale furs closes the entrance again; before looking at me he focuses on the embers, far more interesting to him than I was.

Why is it so hard for me to say 'the man'? His emotion by the fire, his care for me were very human. His baldness suggested the blood of a white man. But something about him frightened me. More than anything, his refusal to speak.

With him I changed. Usually spontaneous, I became cunning. Usually courageous, I started to fear. Usually grateful, I was forced into resentment.

Two more memories. The days when he smoked the pieces of mule snatched from the condors, the taste of mush he fed me with. When I recovered, I found out the mush was mule meat he had chewed.

Months passed. I came to know his scowling light-blue eyes, close-set by his beaky red nose. A giant crouched before the fire. I wanted to make him talk, so I told stories, I sang, I even recited ten-line verses, but to no effect. Deaf and dumb I thought, but that wasn't it. How many times had I startled him with the sound of my voice, making him turn his back with fury? My struggle was to make him speak, his, to remain silent. Since he couldn't convince me, he once threw a stone at me. Small, but effective enough on my wounds. I accepted his silence. It meant renouncing friendship.

Spanish, I decided. Basque, a mountaineer. A deserter. Or someone like me, a left-over. What made me think so? His Basque appearance, his features. And a certain intuition.

I came to think my uniform was what prevented him from talking. A maggot gnawing on the empire. But up there, what did any of that mean?

It meant nothing. For me, he went against all that was human. Despite having saved me with so much effort, we were enemies. Because of that, because of the silence.

But why did he want to remain so silent?

When he wanted to sleep he disappeared into a corner. I imagined the cave formed an elbow shape; I later confirmed it.

Fear, as if all the evil of the mountain were concentrated in him, made me pretend to be weaker than I was even after I started to recover. Only when he left and all the noise ceased, except the wind and murmurs at those heights, did I have the courage to sit up.

Then I crawled, groaning, understanding that complete health was still far off, and that I had to yield to time and my host in order to escape alive.

Yield, what a word. Yielding for me had always meant talking, saying one's name, telling things to each other.

When I could take a few steps, I saw his bedding, his treasures: the cannon, straps, remains of uniforms, weapons both patriotic and Spanish, the mule's harness, stone tools.

I spent hours and hours alone. He went out to hunt. I understood he did so in anticipation of winter. Winter! I'd been wounded in spring, and already at that time the cold was almost unbearable in the bivouac, let alone on the marches. Winter. I clung to the cave as if it were my mother's womb. Dying is no strange thing. But on the mountain…

Let's jump ahead to the first snowfall.

The cave was deeply cold.

Every time he went out, I sat up. The dizziness was overwhelming, I leaned on the rock. I flexed my arms and legs. Or rather one arm and one leg. The others were stiff as a couple of stakes. I'd sworn to be stronger than them and spent hours rubbing them, forcing them to yield. They resisted, but there was progress. That progress was my fixed idea, the meaning of my days.

A difference in the light made me peek outside. I saw fresh snow. I saw footprints.

Almost round. A cubit in diameter. The toe detached, the rest blurry. Barefoot, biped footprints. To judge by the sinking of the snow, the owner's weight was proportional.

I trembled like a hare. I imagined the monster's sense of smell, my own weakness. I imagined my saviour outside, and me at his mercy. I was about to drag myself away in search of the sabre when the stones at the entrance moved. I backed away towards the coals, prepared to set fire to the blanket as a first defence; but as soon as I made out the hand wrapped in strips of wool, my cunning took precedence, I threw myself on the ground under the blanket, I pretended to sleep.

This time he looked closely at me before checking the fire. It's true I wasn't in the same place as usual, but in that weather it was natural to seek warmth. He wanted to make sure of something about me. His breathing was controlled, not agitated. He had seen the footsteps and now wanted to make sure I was sleeping. He knew about the monster. He was only concerned to know if I knew too.

He shook me. I pretended to wake up although my pulse was leaping. He pointed at my corner. I pointed at the coals. Immediately, so as not to be caught in the trap of speaking in signs, I said:

'Starting today I'm going to sleep by the fire.'

He shook his head, the grey locks of hair on his balding crown sweeping his shoulders. He grabbed the blanket and threw it into my corner.

There followed a time that saw some changes. My legs began to work better, my arm responded. It was something he seemed to be waiting for. He started some blacksmithing work, which in the beginning I didn't understand, using musket barrels as tongs, stones as anvils. And fire, of course. He sewed a pair of bellows out of hides before my eyes without my realising what it was for. I began to admire him.

As a slave-driver, first of all. I had noticed how people from the mountains, people from Europe, worked as if they had no hearts, constantly. He had me at the bellows for thousands of hours. He wanted to turn my cannon into something else. And he did. We did. We made a couple of shovels, or something of the kind.

That reminds me how hard we shovelled snow away.

Sometimes I thought the footsteps had been a hallucination. Sometimes I heard a noise and jumped up to defend myself. I imagined my sabre snapping like a piece of straw in a bear's paws. A mastodon seemed to rush at me, I could see its huge tusks. One day it was furry, another day covered in scales, yet another day a giant that could grab a man in each hand and slice their heads off with one bite. The fire was my plan: I'd throw embers in its eyes to begin with, then right after, a torch at its snout, chest and belly. I could hear its shriek. I could hear it draw back, bent over with claws withdrawn.

I never spoke about him.

Alone, kneading hides, making leather fastenings, sewing and smoking meats (my activity was domestic; my going out was frowned upon), I had time to think. I imagined many things. The light of day keeps us balanced. I lived in shadows. I imagined my man had domesticated the monster and made it hunt for us. I imagined too much. Taking the wind as an excuse I surrounded my bed with stones, projectiles I wanted to have at hand.

That night I jumped towards them. A horrible voice woke me. It cried out with a thousand echoes. The monster. No. The embers gave off a calm light under the dark vaults. Everything was calm. Except that voice and those echoes, that language not spoken by any people, in which recognisable words floated: María Luisa, Cayetano.

My companion was dreaming in Basque.

I got used to so much in that time that growing accustomed to his dreams needed no otherworldly effort. What did come from another world were his voice and his language, those echoes. And the cold.

During one of my inspections I discovered a hole covered with gravel and, very worn-out, the military document of Miguel Cayetano Echeverrigoitía, born in Hornachuelos, Biscay, soldier of the Fourth Infantry of the King's Hunters. How clever I felt. I even laughed. At his mercy, for a moment I felt I was his master.

This awoke in me the urge to talk, after being reduced for so long to monosyllables. It took an unexpected form: I told racy jokes. They had never amused me before; you hear too many of them in the bivouacs. One by one I repeated all those I knew. I meant to wake something in him, I didn't know well what. Laughter. That's it, laughter. Which after words is the most human thing of all (if you except betrayal). I felt that laughter, a smile, could be the dawn of a word. One word and the wall of his madness could fall.

I see him now as I did that night, under the reddish light, a bone from which he's sucking the marrow stuck in his mouth like a flute. He didn't find the jokes funny. His breathing grew agitated. I regretted having possibly stirred his lust. I became silent, and very sad.

I set a date for speaking to him about the monster. 'Tomorrow, at the crack of dawn.'

Dawn is the mountain's cruellest lie. It seems innocent, even beautiful.

But that day there was no dawn. I woke without light. The snow blocked us. No chance of shovelling.

We were buried.

He seemed calm. I decided to be so too. If I had to die it would be with dignity. My only objection was that if it was my fate to die on the mountain, why hadn't it happened before, on the ravine between the cannon and the horseshoe; why go through this relationship in the cave and this healing, just to come to the same end? At least there were no condors, and that was something. There was…

I knew by heart what there was. Provisions, smoked; hanging herbs; piles of fuel. My Basque had worked as hard as a sailor.

I had always trusted I would be out of there before we had to consume certain provisions I had smoked during the summer and fall. Snakes, for example, that my companion had snatched from the condors, by throwing stones deadly as lightning bolts. I faced eating them philosophically, thinking of them as nourishment that would give me strength.

Then began the kind of cohabitation that leads to murder, that of two people who are walled in.

We lived wrapped in furs and clinging to the fire we kept burning in a pit. We wrapped our heads in strips of uniform from different regiments, covered in frost, our eyes not showing; we covered our legs and feet in saddle blankets stuffed with straw and goat hair. Outside the wind was, I don't know, say, like the mountain turned into air, tumbling. We were amoebas in its belly, ready to be evacuated into nothingness.

Maggot of the empire, maggot of liberty, writhing a little longer, but for how long? What for?

And without speaking.

He ruled, he was the master of the house. No objections. What to eat, what to drink, what to make, when to exercise, everything, everything done in silence.

What to drink? Ah, yes. Every meal was completed with a tisane. Mine, I discovered, was only for me. It had a bitter taste, the roots of a blackish vegetable.

It took me a while to realise it was a narcotic. I began to sleep a lot and would wake up feeling heavy, still dreaming. I dreamt, I went about drowsy all day. Better this way, I thought. Even the cries of 'María Luisa, Cayetano!' no longer woke me.

I was asleep the night the monster entered the cave. Asleep the hours it took him to dig away the snow outside, the days it took to reach the entrance, asleep when it dragged aside the rocks to open a path. The wind did not put out the fire. We didn't die of cold. Because a hand had been there to surround the embers with stones, close the opening from the inside, let the monster out, and close the rocks again. The hand of an accomplice of the monster.

I noticed the changes the next day. Light came through the cracks, a wall of stones circled the fire, the rocks at the entrance were arranged in a different way. And there was a certain smell.

My waking was observed with such attention that I understood: it was life or death. I decided to be an idiot.

I exulted, 'Ah! The snow outside has melted!'

The alliance of Don Miguel Cayetano Echeverrigoitía with a monster of an unknown species was enough to erase the effects of his narcotic. I channelled my exaltation. Bending over the stones I had been striking for weeks to get something like an axe, I forced my nervous system into a rhythm as regular as the blows. But my companion was perceptive and able to notice the change.

I realised, as if I saw it written in letters on the wall, that my death had been decreed, that everything depended on my ability to pretend. That my axe, the hides I had kneaded and sewed, the meats I had smoked, my own flesh, to be smoked, would be used for the survival of the one who had saved me. The despotism of winter was about to reveal its secret. My life depended on that discovery. I decided to delay it, to be the most idiotic of idiots.

But since curiosity is common in idiots and in others, I decided not to drink the tisane. For this, I counted on my companion's modesty, which made him turn his back as soon as one went towards the pit and the heap of sandstone. There my tea met its end, and its steam was no different from what usually came from that place.

I pretended to feel the greatest drowsiness, I lay down to sleep. And I did sleep, just as I did all the nights that followed, because I had no more news of the monster. I almost even forgot it existed. It began to seem another hallucination.

But it wasn't possible to forget everything. Through heavy shovelling we kept open the excavation that had led it to our door. I felt as if I'd die of fatigue. And the white immensity outside made me feel as if I'd die of sorrow. Not to ask about the miracle that had opened that gap was almost, almost suicide.

I made a comment about the good luck that had brought that 'melting'. It produced a ferocious, attentive stare. Leaning over my shovel, I seemed innocent. My wretched condition as a man of the plains could explain away most things.

Did I say that curiosity is common to many? Yes it is. Even to monsters.

My man had made something like rackets for his feet. He managed to go outside without going far, so that a great snowfall wouldn't cut him off from the cave. Which meant I went back to spending my hours alone. Such relief.

I was alone, polishing my axe, when I felt I was being observed. Slowly my hairs stood up on end, but I continued my task. I thought maybe the Basque, in a twist of his madness, had resolved to kill me. Or maybe…

Under the pretence of adding fuel to the fire, I approached the door and glanced out. Something on the other side of the rocks was peeking inside. Something that covered more cracks of light than a man would, even with furs, even with a turban. A huge shadow.

I brought the torches. I brought a musket with a bayonet that was near the Basque's bed. I brought a shovel and filled it with embers. I surrounded myself with stones.

Then the shadow disappeared. The sad light from outside came back in through the cracks.

I decided: let's end this rat's life. Let's fight; let's fight.

And I started to think. Thought, as it does for so many, made me a sceptic. Even if I did kill the monster, and if I killed my benefactor, what could I do in that place in winter? I would have to wait for the thaw before making a move.

Very well, I would wait.

Now comes the night the monster got in. A blast of cold woke me. I saw a furry silhouette make its way towards the Basque's corner.

I woke up. On hearing the sound of a voice, my companion's, I stifled what had almost been a cry of alarm. He whispered a curt command. Then... may God forgive me... those grunts, what can I say about them? What can I say of the moon that illuminated the giant being as it withdrew, breasts drooping over its swollen, yes, pregnant, belly? It was a female.

As far as life starting from that night goes, I will say: weapon in hand, back to the wall, we ate without speaking, without gestures. The secret was stronger than any alliance. I developed a sympathy for that one who did not want to return to the world of the word, the great exile, who to his shame had succumbed to compassion for someone like him. That's how things were.

That's how things were until the thaw.

Until the sound of cavalry, of a bugle in a gorge below.

I jumped up, frantic. I moved my arms. Then I saw the flag, red and gold. The king's flag.

Something grabbed me by the shoulders. It wasn't the monster, although it seemed so from its strength. My companion, his tiny eyes glassy under the sun, tucked a slip of paper into my hand: his registration document. Then he pushed me over the cliff, same as my mule.

So I fell unconscious among the king's troops, maggots of liberty, and I, a maggot of empire. I transformed into Miguel Cayetano Echeverrigoitía, native of Biscay, dressed in furs and mute for reasons of prudence, though not deaf, as my companions noticed and commented upon.

Tied to the back of a mule, my leg in a splint, exhausted, I knew the precipices, ravines, caverns and rock faces were being left behind. That was all I asked for.

Then a cry was heard. The strangest, the most terrible. It echoed up there. It hit the abyss, bounced and rebounded.

My Andalusian companions looked at one another, trembling. An Aragonese artilleryman murmured:

'The Irrintzi...'

I had heard about that. It was the cry of the Basques.

The suspicions began afterwards. For the moment they remained silent.

'What is it celebrating?' a young man next to me asked.

Silent, I said to myself, 'A new race.'

I let out a hideous laugh.

But all of them thought I was mad anyway.

A NEW SCIENCE

I WILL TELL YOU what I was able to discover.

It was 1942. The year Silvina Ocampo published her *Epitaphs for Twelve Chinese Clouds*. A tall melancholy man wanted to talk with her. A linotypist. By chance he had seen the galley proofs of the poems on a table. The man had a cough, as many typesetters do; soon he gave up his attempt. It was a fantasy, but understandable if you consider the task to which he had dedicated his life.

The man who told me these things in a basement room near the river was his successor.

The task looked like a bunch of papers, some of them yellowing. Arturo Manteiga, the linotypist, and Claudio Sánchez, the one talking to me, had been the third and fourth ones to inherit it.

The yellowest part began with a title page that featured decorations of the finest calligraphy. They were in the author's own hand. Surrounded by the decorations, the name, date and title of the work could be seen.

Giacomo Pizzinelli. 1852. *The Influence of Clouds on History.*

Pizzinelli had made observations for thirty-seven years. Day after day he had described the shapes of the clouds and their progress, and day after day from 1852 to 1889 he had noted the variations of politics and the changes of mood in the elite and the people, as far as possible.

In the beginning he limited himself to his city, Verona. Turin was the second step. He followed the events. He could draw the clouds floating on 24 May 1856, when the Austrians withdrew from Tuscany, and those on 17 March 1861, during the proclamation of the Kingdom of Italy.

Thanks to a recommendation, he came here in 1889 as a railway engineer. Within a month, he died in Concordia. In bed, in between bouts of fever, he managed to win a disciple.

Very pale, making notes in the light of the kerosene lamp, José Manteiga decided to do him justice. He was a young Spanish apothecary. It took him some time to complete the sale of his business. He arrived in Buenos Aires on 1 January 1890. He drew the clouds above the Park during the shoot-out between troops and revolutionaries. With great trembling he confirmed that their shapes coincided with the ones recorded by Pizzinelli in Paris in April 1871, the days of the Commune.

He decided to devote himself to a point that had worried Pizzinelli. The shape of the clouds depends on distance from the sea, humidity, wind, temperature and hemisphere. But to what degree was the action of the clouds not merely a product of atmospheric conditions, of which clouds constituted only the visible sign?

To study this problem he appealed to correspondents, contacted two meteorologists in Italy, made the acquaintance of a friend in Spain and an expert working for the army in Buenos Aires. In addition he completed the basic morphology established by Pizzinelli. The *Catalogue of Cloud Shapes, with Possible Historical, Political and Economic Consequences* was composed of four hundred analytic sketches.

José Manteiga continued his work until 1920. Then a burst blood vessel immobilised him for a long period. He died without recovering his speech.

At that point the new science had sixty-eight years of uninterrupted studies. In its archive: 1,267 watercolours, charcoal drawings and pencil sketches by Pizzinelli; 4,305 pencil drawings, gouaches and photos by José Manteiga. In addition there were notes taken by both of them, in different handwriting, illustrated reports from Manteiga's correspondents and folders of journalistic clippings with comments, ranging from 1852 to 1920. If one analysed them, astonishing coincidences could be noticed.

Arturo Manteiga had been his adopted father's assistant since childhood. In his final years, his photographer. Pizzinelli had already discovered in 1852 that history always changes during the night, although luckily or unluckily citizens only notice those changes when they wake up. Arturo learned to photograph nocturnal clouds.

Manteiga, Arturo, renounced marriage. He renounced everything so as to continue with his task. But the yields of typesetting are few, the cost of photography high.

Here the new science records the entrance of a woman: Nora. The new science has not recorded her surname. She was the manager of a fashion house, a bit fat and good-natured, according to a photo snapped with Arturo in Lezama Park. For nine years she and Arturo loved one other. Afterwards she married the owner of a pasta factory. This was no betrayal of the cloud science. The pasta man never knew about the part of his dividends that went to support Arturo's research. Arturo could rely on Nora's help, her car, her capacity for observation.

In those outstandingly tidy folders, the clouds that determined the 1943 coup were recorded. When examined, they turned out to be near twins of the ones from 6 September 1930, when the cadets from the Military Academy advanced towards the capital. Afterwards Arturo could record and analyse the coincidence between the clouds presiding over the popular movements of 1916 and 1945.

Determined, I said. Presided over, I said. Yes.

Pizzinelli's and José Manteiga's great concern had been resolved by Arturo.

It's clouds themselves, not the mere factors that form them, that act on the collective events of humanity. They combine them, decide them, precipitate them.

This was made clear. Established.

How?

I must appeal here to my lack of knowledge. In the basement near the river, Claudio Sánchez, the last disciple, showed me pages covered in numbers. I don't understand anything about numbers. But if I can trust my memory, I would say the explanation was more or less like this: it's true that clouds result from a combination of factors. At the same time, clouds are more than those factors. They possess an essential energy, they make history.

I was twenty-three years old the day of the interview. It was in July 1954. It was cold and humid. That young man in front of me was explaining these things. He was fat, studious and poor. The archive spilled across the table seemed the quintessence of innumerable lives.

The man was Nora's godson. He had visited her every Sunday as a child, then orphanhood had made him a regular of her house. And loved by her. He inherited her anxieties. Later he would inherit the noodle factory.

Claudio Sánchez. The studies of Pizzinelli and the Manteigas, José and Arturo, acquired the appearance of novelty with him. That afternoon I could see two notebooks. *Historical conjectures*, they were titled. They described, on strictly scientific bases, the clouds on the day of Caesar's assassination, the clouds of Napoleon's coronation, the clouds of Maipú, of Caseros.

It was in that basement, in that cold, in that July 1954, that I came to learn what I am telling.

Like art, science doesn't often concern itself with means.

Claudio had a project.

A century and two years of continuous studies. Conclusive proofs. No publication. This is how Claudio Sánchez summarised the state of the new science. He became indignant. Was the unconscious worth more than the sky? Was capital worth more than the sky? An impressive anger overcame him.

And since science doesn't concern itself with means, and since a dignified publication was urgently needed, Claudio did not hesitate. He would resort to the government.

His girlfriend knew a Franciscan whose political sermons made people talk. The Franciscan, sincerely comparing those in power with saints, had found a path towards those in power. And just as they say, love awakens love.

That Franciscan responded to Claudio Sánchez with an extraordinary enthusiasm. The ideas of the treatise on celestial science in politics mirrored those of a ruling political government that compared itself with the saints. The order would take care of the publication. Ten tomes. Photographs in colour, biographies of the founders of the new science. Everything. Guaranteed.

I must say I did nothing to dissuade Claudio Sánchez. Anyway, it was time for the world to know of that discovery. In any case, my interview was casual on that cold day in July 1954.

I didn't learn much about Claudio Sánchez then. I mean, I learned two things.

The following year, in July 1955, when some youths sent by the government set fire to churches, a man rushed to rescue something from the bonfire of the church of San Francisco. As we know, nothing was saved from San Francisco. The police pulled out the man, and put him in jail. When the government changed, they wanted to honour him as a hero.

In 1975 a television programme presented an obese, asthmatic man, owner of a chain of pasta factories. He explained what took up most of his free time, of which he had a great deal. For a while this appearance fed the sense of humour of the country. The man photographed and classified clouds. It was Claudio Sánchez.

GEORGETTE AND THE GENERAL

T HIS STORY TELLS how a good thought transformed an Eden into a desert.

The desert can be seen by anyone who sticks his head out the train window a few stations after Chajáes.

I saw the Eden in my childhood. The white house, the garden. Plane trees with mottled trunks reaching down to the water. Its balcony, now missing, and its doors, no longer there. That care and attention made one think less of a country establishment than of the sewing box of a tidy owner. Someone asked whom it belonged to. Someone replied.

Georgette was a young girl General Narváez brought back from France. All things French were the rage. From a trip one had to bring back soaps, clothes, books, cooks, shoes, perfumes, pianos, cheeses, hats, sheets, governesses, gloves, wines, and if you could afford it, a girl. Nowadays you can get most of that here rather easily.

She was especially charming, not only because of her dimples but also because everything seemed well to her. She must have smiled at the thought of setting up in the countryside. The inevitable can also be accepted without smiling.

The general spent most of the year making the estate, now famous, into something magnificent. The avenues are now so beautiful that seeing them makes you want to cry. Even the birds there look down on the others without anybody contesting that right. To be frank, that estate is the best monument to the general's glory. Because of the bronze statues and the blue enamel signs bearing his name in streets throughout the country, I won't mention it. In any case, the estate would play a small role in this story, were it not that Georgette's house was three leagues away from there. Just over an hour at a gallop.

She settled in with a flurry of trunks. What she thought of such a big plain, we don't know. She knew the beef-steaks and the monuments to the national heroes. She must have understood.

The general was the most civilised of men. He would have considered the slightest error in his French an unforgivable defeat. They made him suffer. Laughing, she would correct him. Nothing serious, subtleties. They had such a good time together, as if they had never left Paris.

Georgette's little house trailed beside the big ranch like a feather left behind by a swan while swimming. Seen from above, as the storks saw them every day, they made one think of a white foal following its mother. Seen from the ground, they looked less related to each other. An enormous colourful whale sleeping in the sun, and a rowboat. A continent populated with different races, and an island.

Once idle, Georgette became active. The first yield of eggs gave origin to a certain *omelette surprise* that inspired risqué jokes. She invented flower arrangements for the house. If anyone, in summer, serves cherries mixed with jasmine, it should be known that she did too.

Watching her work, the general called her *ma petite abeille*. When he came from the train he brought her gifts; she was happy. When he came from the ranch, he talked to her about maples, poplars and alders; it bored her. But no one hid boredom better. Chin on her hand, eyes bright, she thought about other things. Later he recounted memories of standard-bearer grandparents in the Andes, and of the general himself devastating the Indians. She remembered: he was a hero. Her face lit up.

Were it not for Obarrio, it would have been paradise. Obarrio had served under the general and stood to attention when he spoke to him. His hair hung down to his shoulders, and he wore a headband and *chiripá* trousers. He was Georgette's overseer. Although she had trusted men since childhood, she couldn't look at him without fright. The general had told her how, when the battle of Los Pasos had ended, he had stayed on to observe the plain from horseback: the dead, the horses without owners, noises. He had seen a man on foot among the remains and thought it must be a thief. The man leaned over the fallen, pulled up their heads by the hair, slit their throats. Once the task was accomplished he mounted his horse and left. It was Obarrio.

It was useless for the general to explain to Georgette what a gaucho was. It was useless for her to ask for another overseer. Obarrio often scratched his arm. She had no doubt it was the spilled blood that stung him. She never managed to understand that the throats her overseer had slashed had not deserved any further thoughts from him.

The six o'clock train often brought her boxes with bows. Blouses appeared, petticoats with ribbons, a shawl. The wind filled the house with the smell of sheep. She smiled in front of the mirror.

The first challenge to her reign happened one summer. The general's family settled at the ranch. She spent days and nights alone. Sometimes she was able to see him still. He came at sunset smelling of eau de cologne.

When he was a minister she didn't see him for months. When he started the presidential campaign she didn't see him any more. The faithful, allies, flatterers arrived at the station by the dozen. One night, a group drunk on champagne spun its cart onto the track leading to her house, and offered her the most unpleasant serenade. Obarrio turned the carthorses back, and chased them away with his riding crop. Georgette didn't go out for days.

The general's presidency was brilliant. But Georgette was not interested in politics.

She grew fat. That curl that always escaped from her coiffure stopped escaping. Sometimes, sitting before the piano, she let sound a note.

She dedicated herself to order. A speck of dust was a drama.

The cook stayed behind. So did Obarrio. Once a year he left. Where to? To drink blood in the land of Indians, according to the cook. What blood? Georgette enquired trembling. Fresh blood from mares, the kind that pulses to the mouth from the neck in a stream that grows and shrinks with the beat of the heart. A month later Obarrio would come back, greet everybody, let his horses free. He would go back to work.

Georgette suffered from fainting spells. She would have the town doctor called. The farmhand would leave at a gallop. Fever overtook her. The boy from the pharmacy arrived on a chestnut horse, the cupping glasses clinking in the saddlebag. Both the doctor and the boy attended diligently, both left with their heads full of dreams.

Seated on a bench in the garden, she started to speak in French. One day she raised her eyes and saw the cut-throat of Los Pasos before her. A black toe emerged from his raw horsehide boots. He asked for a *cerisette*. He carried a lamb in his arms, which he offered her to raise. She didn't understand his gaucho lisp. He didn't understand French.

She died one afternoon in her imperial bed. The taffeta quilt was the same pink as the setting sun. Her ghost rose up. It saw her, hair dishevelled, asleep. It saw the house, the piano, the kitchen. It saw the horses on the hitching rail. It saw a diamond, a star, a lily – or thought it had seen them. It was Obarrio's love. Love for her.

Floating in the house she inspected the wardrobes, the remaining flowers. A longing to leave, an anxiety to stay, she hung about uneasily, her fate in limbo. She trembled like the cork on an invisible thread in an invisible water.

The president of the Republic was playing croquet with his daughter. It was his month of vacation. Beneath the trees a girl smiled, dimples that shifted in the lights and shadows of the straw hat. She was blonde. A curl escaped from her coiffure; like a swarm of bees, a memory of kisses surrounded her. The general ran beneath the branches. The shout of one daughter stopped him. He turned back with an ecstatic smile. He was about to fall into a canal made deep by the rains.

The general's decadence began. From that moment he lost the steel quality of his mind. In conference with the governors he would interrupt to ask for a liquor bonbon. The country expected a government comparable to the first one. The vice president made an effort to please him. Nothing turned out as it should have. Anyway, the general had already entered history. And history didn't blame him for that end.

No one knew Georgette's surname. Even the general had forgotten it. On the tomb only Georgette was written, and a date.

She remained alone, floating through the house and the garden. Her passion for order persisted. The house took on an abnormal splendour. Not a feather was carried away by the wind, not a leaf entered through the window of the salon for years. Rumours spread, staff could not be found. The Eden lingered on.

Half a century came to an end when one of the general's daughters, the one who had run after him that day playing croquet, turned eighty. Because of that, she had a good thought. She ordered a mass for all living and dead members of the de Narváez family, as for all those related to it. The merits of a mass are infinite. The benefits met and exceeded the expectations. They reached further than the general's daughter had imagined. They reached the farmhands who had dug the holes for the trees of his ranch, the Indians he had exterminated and the soldiers he had commanded. They reached allies and enemies. They reached Obarrio, the cook, the town doctor and the boy from the pharmacy. They reached me, the one telling you all this, and you, the ones reading it. They reached Georgette.

That blessing fell on her soul. Her uneasiness shattered like a glass. A slit seemed to appear. Through which she slipped. And she entered peace.

The house finally let go. The leaves could move again over the avenues, the gazebo rotted, wasps settled on the chandeliers. The balcony collapsed; it lost its doors. The Eden turned into desert.

There it remains. It can be seen by anyone who sticks his head out the train window a few stations after Chajáes.

THINGS HAPPEN

ONCE UPON A TIME there was a pensioner with a garden in Lanús. He had been head of personnel at a state-owned company.

His garden was the admiration and envy of all Lanús. That's a zone that, as everyone knows, lacks water two days out of three. The neighbourhood writes notes of protest, and the first to sign them has always been the pensioner with the garden.

The usual way was this: the neighbour who most liked complaining would arrive with his document in hand. He would find the pensioner kneeling under the rose bushes, or covering the paths with white pebbles, or passing a rake over a circle of lawn which looked like, let's say, an emerald. Ant poisons, fertilisers and tools could be seen in the green shed through a sheet of fibreglass. And there, standing up, almost without taking off his straw hat or wiping the mud from his fingers, the pensioner would add his signature, a single flourish, just as he had signed so often in his days as a director.

One morning he woke up. The smell of his garden was missing. Was it raining? The pleasant drip-drip of water wasn't sounding against his window either. Uneasy, he went outside. He found himself in the middle of the sea.

A green wave rocked the garden. A strong wind had knocked down the scarecrow.

He fell to the ground. When he regained his strength, he lifted his face. Again, he saw himself navigating in the sea. Once again he fell prostrate to the ground.

He noticed, one of the times he stood up, that foam was sprinkling the jasmines on his fence, neatly painted white. In desperation, he looked for a tarp he kept in case of hail and tried to cover them. It was difficult. He barged ahead, clinging to the small fence not meant to serve as a railing. He tied the tarp to the rail and to some wooden pickets stuck in the earth. He worked with dedication, with rage.

Dizzy, soaked, he thought of taking a warm shower. But he realised the water in his tank was limited. He would need it for his plants, to drink.

Nonsense. He was dreaming. He threw himself on the bed and closed his eyes.

He dreamed he was in his office, a frequent dream of his. An employee was asking for leave: his wife was dying. Forty-eight hours, he would tell him. The employee left, tears of frustration splashing the lenses of his glasses. Those tears were falling on the face of the personnel director.

No, they weren't tears. The wind had changed, and there was condensation on the open glass of the window, falling on him in drops.

He sat up. Was it true then? The scene before him seemed to be dancing. Clinging to the walls, he went out.

It was true.

The garden, veering slowly, was changing course. Its prow pointed towards a vast expanse identical to the one surrounding him on all sides.

The rose bushes leaned their chubby cheeks towards him, as if asking for help. He rinsed them with fresh water, sobbing in their ears.

But he was hungry. He went to the pantry. There was instant coffee and several cans of tongue, mackerel, milk powder. He hated all that. They were gifts from his sister, who was married to an employee of a meat-packing firm.

Because, as he had clearly stated the morning she arrived – loaded, breathless, the marks of the bag handles on her hands – before making gifts one should enquire about the tastes of others. He followed the principles of veganism, with occasional exceptions for yogurt and cheese without salt. Yet his sister had left that packet.

Cans. And how helpful they were now. With a groan, he opened one.

How long would this last?

Or maybe he was crazy. Maybe he only thought he was in the sea, while his neighbours were looking over the fence at him with pity. It was easy to imagine their conjectures: so many hours in the sun, dedicated to his plants... Or maybe he was in an insane asylum now, hallucinating? Maybe the drops he believed were falling on him were injections?

Whatever the case, there he was. He saw the sea through the windows, green and sparkling now that the sun was up.

The sun! He got up to look at his grass. Bright emerald still, and fresh. But for how long?

Desperation made him burst out in shrieks.

At sunset he took up the newspaper he had been reading the day before. Football, movies, comic strips. How far away everything seemed now. He checked the date. He made an almanac on the last page of a seed catalogue.

The only thing left now was to sleep. Night had fallen. Outside, that murmur. Inside, the rocking motion.

Days, night, mornings followed.

The first to die were the carnations. They trembled, dried up, brown. The roses saw their petals fly over the desert. Then their stalks twisted into spirals. The grass died in patches. All that was left was a bare circle of earth with bits of straw. They eventually flew away too.

The fence, tarp and jasmines fell heavily in the sea with crash.

The pensioner attempted to distract himself. He turned on the television. But it transmitted wavy lines that reminded him too much of the surrounding undulations. He went on noting down each day in his almanac. He examined the water tank. He cursed heaven that he lived in West Lanús. The usual lack of water was reflected in the tank three-quarters empty. The terror of thirst started to obsess him.

Looking for some positive side to his situation, he told himself that the weather was steady, and that the waves would lead him somewhere.

But then the calm came.

The anxieties of the calm have already been written about too well. The loss of hope for a port, provisions and water running out, the glowing of strange presences, the agony.

Sweat trickled down the pensioner's bald head in his destroyed garden. He had gathered the white pebbles in two flowerpots, which he kept in the kitchen, but outside, the flowerbed's design now appeared to him like a laugh without teeth.

On the tenth day of the calm, a loud racket set the garden in motion. The sea rushed forward. There was a collapse.

The end! he thought, clinging to the dry trunk of a shrub. As in a fit, he recalled a television programme. The winner, a prodigy of a boy, had said that the ancients believed in a flat world with a waterfall at the edge. The conductor handed him a prize, and everyone laughed at the ancients.

'Here we are!' he thought in despair, dragged with the house and garden into the depths. A circular current held them while the entire sea made the sound of regurgitation.

A monster appeared. It had dripping scales and looked extremely content. Its head brushed the low storm clouds. Limp vegetation hung from its mouth.

The fear was unimaginable. Of the fear he felt, I will only say: it was like being dead: no pulse, on the ground. An image crossed his mind. He had once seen a photo of two trains crashing on the Lanús line. One of them stood vertical.

Tall as a hundred trains, the sea serpent lifted her body into the air, and enjoyed the view of infinite sea. That view made her feel like moving. She didn't see the chalet, too close and slightly behind: she was sated, too.

Parts of her body rose from the water as she moved away, while others sank into the waves, and the pensioner, his garden and his house spun in the whirlpools, until he felt the atoms of his self starting to split.

This happened on the thirtieth day of navigation.

*

By that time he had decided to protect the glass of the windows. Any cracks would be serious. The house was his refuge. He closed the shutters and got used to walking around in the dark inside. It was a relief.

Outside the sun bludgeoned the garden. Dressed from head to toe, in a hat and gardening gloves so as not to see his flesh reduced to shreds, he tried to fish. Without a fence, it was a dangerous task. He tied himself to the grass tap and used tinned food as bait. He spent days making hooks.

He discovered that sometimes he did catch something. He promised himself he would eat that, no matter what it was. If a whole day passed without a catch he would open a can. It must be said that all sorts of beings crawled and throbbed in the garden, tossed into it by the waves or arriving by personal initiative. They spared him the effort of fishing. He flung them into a cooking pot. Some gave him terrible skin rashes. Others gave him dyspepsia. Still others had no effect. Fearing for his fuel supply, he cooked several dishes at a time in the oven. He got used to cold soup. But seafood makes you thirsty. What made him most anxious was the decreasing water supply.

One day two seabirds landed on the television antenna. Out of habit he insulted them, waving his arms. Go away from my fields. In the middle of the gesture he stopped. A bird means land.

'Land!' he shouted, sinking to his knees, his voice cracking in a thousand tones.

There was no land in sight. The birds were of an unknown dark-red colour. But he didn't notice it. Seeing that his fuss had scared them off he begged, 'Stay!'

He had to watch them move slowly towards the east.

He kept his eyes fixed in that direction. A waste of a morning. Better to lack hope than to gain and lose it. He made it into the house, threw himself into bed and cried.

In the afternoon he looked again. He thought he was dying. He wetted his head. He saw something like a mountain.

And what if he passed it, in this aimless navigation beyond his control? But it was coming nearer.

At sundown the light grazed until it hit a blackish-red crag, like a blood clot. Foam tossed against the shoals.

No gesture, no human sound came from it. If carefully observed, it seemed to move, like a dead rat covered in flies. Seabirds covered it. Their caws seemed like the voice of that stone.

The pensioner fell on his knees, stretched his arms towards the crag, cried out. He looked for a bed sheet and waved it frantically, begging for help. Nothing.

But, actually, yes. With the sinking of the sun, the crag seemed to be made of enormous faces, just like those he had seen in movies, some of America's national heroes carved in a mountain. In the movie they had seemed magnificent. But not here. Maybe because of the birds' droppings or because of the reef fog, those men's and women's faces looked as if they had a cold, with runny noses, teary, or dribbling. He screamed until he almost lost his voice, his strength, his life.

When the sun set, he got terrified. Despite his fear of the reef, he shut himself in the house.

What to do now? Not sleep. He looked for some magazines he kept under the bed.

His neighbour on the left in Lanús, a poor thing contented with geraniums in flowerpots, belonged to a Protestant sect. He often chatted him up over the fence, praising his garden, though his real intention was to convert him. Once a month, he would produce a publication from under his arm as he took his leave and say, 'Maybe this will keep you entertained.'

That was enough to irritate him. But since those who work with fertilisers and phosphates need to have papers at hand, he kept the magazines. He would use them when he had to wrap up waste, satisfied that the neighbour could sometimes see his pages in the rubbish bin.

What to do, tonight? He tried to focus on the humour section. A healthy humour. Nothing about alcoholism or adultery. Almost always something about dogs or cats. Impossible to understand, with that crag the colour of a blood clot, those reefs, birds, and faces so close in the night.

He looked out. He tried to see something, to hear the noise from the cliffs. Nothing.

The inconvenience of bad journalism is that while reading it, you think of something else. He had suffered when he retired. What a personnel director he had been! The employee called in sick. I hope you get better, he would say in an unforgettable way. He would send the company doctor. What a doctor he was. They had an agreement. Forty-eight hours. Get better. Or die.

He always liked asking his employees their political affiliation. They swallowed bile. The official badge on the dissidents' lapels provided him with great entertainment for a while.

The effect of bad journalism: he fell asleep in the armchair.

A heavy wind began to blow at that hour. The house shook. The sea became a field of waves at play, tossing house, garden and pensioner about, tumbling them from bed to table, from armchair to door.

He heard the antenna of the television as it tore away, bounced off the roof with a metallic goodbye, disappeared into the air.

A shutter's corroded hinges collapsed. The window-pane was uncovered. Light entered through it, and he saw the waves, transparent, covering the sky, licking the sides of the house, filtering through the joints of the windows.

He crawled. He looked for a can of insect glue. He smeared it on the window joints, but water entered anyway, stretching the glue into icicles, dripping down their tips.

Five days of wind. Five days without eating, without making notes in his calendar, clinging to a leg of the bed.

He didn't have the strength to open the door. Trembling, he unsealed a can of sardines. Somehow recovered, he started to make his way outside. He gave a shout.

The garden was a palm underwater. The only part jutting out was on the other side, the part that used to border the Protestant neighbour, a slightly raised section made of brick, where he used to keep clay pots with flowers and flowerbeds. Between the house and that section, the garden looked like a pool crossed by silvery schools of fish.

All around, bare sea stretching towards the horizon.

He didn't have a single tear left. Not a hair remained on his head to yank out. A beard he did have, long and tangled. His electric razor had broken during the first days of navigation.

Does God exist? he wondered. It's true he had prayed at moments of excessive horror, like the night of the crag. His mother had once taught him how. And in a pamphlet he had read the story of the lost man in the Himalayas who had survived thanks to meat extract and prayers. But what prayers were those? And what meat extract?

Let's see, what kind of a situation was this? How could a human being ever anticipate a risk like that? He could prove it: no insurance company would have this in its programme.

He had never insured his life. He didn't think it fair for his sister and brother-in-law to benefit from his death. But if a clause about a similar situation did exist, when he returned, he would…

Return!

Would he return?

He covered his ears with his hands and yelled for a long time.

To calm himself he made a plan of action. First of all, he would have to fish through the window. Then, he would write down his story. Good, but he lacked white paper. He looked around the house. Brown paper lined the cupboard drawers and shelves. That was something. With tiny handwriting… After all, all this might end one day… No. Illusions do harm.

He sat down to write. He wrote the date. 'An impeccable employee, Category J4, in the General Direction of Automotive Personnel and Statistics at the Ministry of Internal Revenue between the years 1928 and 1962, with only two absences for family grief in all my years of service, I retired on 24 March of...'

A voice spoke hoarsely behind his back.

His pencil fell onto the paper. A stiffness immobilised him from the back of his neck to his heels.

He heard it again, panting, a splash. It said, 'My refuge...'

He forced himself to turn around. Clinging to the brick border of the raised part of the garden was a man dripping with water, his face transfigured by hope, his hat squashed. His eyes were fixed on the name of the house, written with cursive letters on a sign on the roof. All of a sudden the pensioner remembered it: My Refuge.

Standing on his doorstep unmoving, not a sound in his throat, he looked at him.

The man saw him. His happiness grew. He panted, as if he had arrived swimming. Grabbing hold of the bricks, he hoisted himself up.

With a crunch of putrefaction, the garden yielded under his weight like a moist biscuit. The brick part went down first, dragging the man along with it. Half the garden followed, tipping vertically as it capsized, disappearing into the vortex.

The pensioner sat down on his doorstep. He pulled his knees to his chest, pressed his face against his fists. He sobbed. As he himself defined it afterwards, it was a nervous breakdown. Once it was over, he opened his eyes little by little. The garden ended in the middle of what had once been a circle of lawn. Maybe because the brick part was gone, it no longer held water. It emerged sloping towards the house.

That man… There was no land, no ship, no lifeboat or log in sight. Where had he come from?

For days and nights, that face transformed by hope, the crunch of the garden as it broke, the disappearance into bubbles remained before his eyes.

He couldn't eat, fish or move. He spent his time lying in bed, staring at the roof that mirrored the reflections of the sea.

And the thirst began. He held it off for a time thanks to the melted ice cubes in the refrigerator. He followed these with the toilet water tank. Later he found himself licking the inside of the refrigerator. Later he found himself licking the toilet bowl.

Later, like a madman, dry tongue hanging out like a hide, he found himself running in circles, sticking his lips to a humid bar of iron covered in salt, wiping them with horror, trying to drink seawater and vomiting, slashing an arm to suck his own blood.

Not a single memory or dream or idea in him except that of fresh water to drink. He looked at the clouds like a calf looks at an udder for the morning milking, something set aside for another purpose. What about him? Oh, clouds.

At last it rained. It was night. He burned with fever on the floor of his bedroom. He heard the drops. He thought he was delirious but he crawled outside.

It was raining! Crying, laughing, naked, he let himself get soaked, mouth open. Water ran over his ears, filled his eyes. He licked himself; he squeezed his beard into his mouth. He brought out jars, pans, pots, cans, bottles.

When morning came it was raining, and it carried on raining. The sloping garden let a bittersweet cascade run towards the house, which he didn't take for granted either. Oh, water. Oh, rain.

There followed a period during which he tried to write down his experiences. It wasn't easy, but a kind of serenity filled him as he gave those events form. In the beginning he struggled with the words. No sea, serpent, wind, red crag or thirst had ever appeared in the writings he had read or written in his life.

That word, life, stopped him. Was he alive?

Or dead?

He tried to remember ideas he had heard heard about death. Nothing similar to this. Whereas concerning life… It's true that some days, for instance when he had caught a beautiful fleshy fish after waiting seven or ten hours, he had felt more alive than he had ever been. And when the rain running into his eyes and mouth ended his long thirst, didn't that feel different from the glass of mineral water a clerk brought to his office every day at 11.10?

Yes, but enough. Enough. Alive or dead, he demanded an explanation. He wanted peace. He needed certainty. Silence. Rest.

The sea in those days was the colour of mustard. He had heard about plankton. He hoped it wasn't plankton, since many said it's what whales eat.

The colour of mustard. A roasted turkey on a white tablecloth. Sauce steaming in the sauceboat. Chestnuts and plums and pine nuts in the filling. Walnuts and almonds in a plate. A cake with a silk ribbon. Cider. It was Christmas. Who, at that table? A woman in a long dress, a girl with braids. In the courtyard the neighbours toasted. He had the right to eat. He reached out his hand, pushing the girl. Something hit his fingers. He had collided against the fibreglass panel that had once sheltered his ant poisons, which had fallen after the great wind.

So they are hallucinations, he told himself. Let's write.

'Between the years 1928 and 1962, only two absences for family mourning, that is, in thirty-four years. The first period of mourning was motivated by the passing of my mother, and the second by that of my wife, fifteen months after our marriage, which had been celebrated during the days of leave in 1935 when the building was closed to clear out rats.'

Looked at attentively, it was the only mistake in his life. A life of order. She… to be honest, he didn't remember her face. On the other side, committing suicide is an infraction of the marital contract. No one had known, luckily.

He went outside to clear his mind.

A line like a streak of tar divided sky from sea on the horizon. It was like the lines that cross accounting books, but with a slight inclination.

Tripping on everything, he thought about turning on the television. No image. But a voice, perhaps female, interrupted by electrical discharges, said incomprehensible things.

'Land!' he yelled for the second time on his trip. 'Land!'

His own yelp frightened him. He waited, eyes fixed on the line. It managed to turn into a stripe; the inclination began to seem like a mountain range. He didn't like the mass of material, shiny as lacquer. He couldn't wait any longer.

He took a bed sheet and alcohol, went to the roof, and waved a fiery flag until the flames singed his beard. He let it go. A breeze carried it spinning into the sea. He lost his balance and fell in the water. Several tiles fell near him.

He came up, gasping. He couldn't swim. He paddled madly towards the house. He remembered the man. 'My Refuge', he read between two splashes.

He managed to get a grip, climb up, stretch himself on the pavement. He allowed no time to rest. On his knees, he looked towards the coast.

It was moving away.

It was them moving away. The house. The garden. Himself.

He roared, hitting the walls, cursed, stamped his feet.

The coast disappeared.

Decisions surface in the morning.

Sitting on a chair in front of the garden, his heart stripped of illusions, he whistled an old tango. He would navigate until the end of time. Without getting upset.

But the flesh is weak. 'End of time' made him think, hopeful, of the bad news of the days previous to his voyage. Each country had its own atomic bomb now. It was therefore possible the planet would explode. Oh, let it explode!

But – was he even on the planet? If not, where was he? If so, on which part of it?

He would not get upset now. He went into the house. He picked up the television. He threw it into the sea.

For a moment he could make it out, recognisable.

Big decisions. During his fall in the water he had seen the house from the outside. He should have imagined it, but never thought about it. A heavy moustache of molluscs and algae surrounded it. Little fish and worms stirred underneath. If that kept growing it would end up sinking him. He got his pruning shears but understood the task was impossible. To prune the edges he would have to get in the water. The lower part was beyond reach anyway. And he didn't dare to step on the garden, in case it detached.

Very well then. He put the pruning shears away.

Fishing and biography, he decided.

Fishing and Navigation, he smiled bitterly. It was the name of a club at Lake Chascomús. He had gone with other bosses in the company to eat silverside fish there in '52. He didn't like silverside, he had said. He didn't like silverside! He was a vegetarian. A vegetarian! The only thing worse would have been to say he didn't like fishing or navigation.

So, here we are, for now. He drummed his fingers on the table, as was his habit at the office. Profession: navigator. He smiled, the corners of his mouth pointing down behind the beard. He had got used to running his hands through it, like a patriarch. It was a highly agreeable sensation. He had untangled it, a task difficult to forget, and now combed it every day. Whereas he trimmed the hair on the back of his neck.

He didn't smell very good, it has to be said. What smell could surprise in that house where washing was abolished from the first day, where fish entered through the window and jumped on the floor, leaving scales? No smell or colour could come as a surprise now. Nothing could.

One invigorating exercise for the navigator's imagination is to mentally paint the abyss below, the depths sheltering mountain ranges; black surroundings, eternal cold. Compared to them, the splashing, the transparency and the light of the surface become pleasant. The precariousness of our suspension is underlined. The disparity of fate becomes obvious when you think of the many bones resting on the sea floor. You begin to meditate on providence, chance, fate.

When watering his garden, how many times had he enjoyed watching the ants struggling in the currents from his hose? Now he thought of them differently. Supposing for a moment a sea god actually existed, the Neptune of the ancients the boy joked about on television, wouldn't he get the same pleasure directing men and their boats as he had spinning the insects, occasionally saving some because of their beauty or harmlessness, in a momentary good mood? Harmless or beautiful from whose point of view? The gardener's. But doubtless there were others.

Philosophy germinates from loneliness. And from fear.

Another habit born of solitude is picking one's nose. He had been prevented from doing it during the years he called normal by the height of the fence, too low to isolate him, and by the fact that his office had been open to anyone with a question. The truly isolated man has all the acts of privacy at his disposal. That is why he elicits mistrust. Since what acts cannot be imagined by fantasy?

They are always the same. Maybe that employee who had broken the onyx inkwell on his desk, hurling the lid to the ceiling – the mark had stayed there forever – or the one who had sent him to hell, apoplectic, and wanted to crush a stamp on his face – luckily there was a bell – or that man thrown out on the street with four children to take care of – et cetera – well, maybe when calm in his house he picked his nose every day. Or the young lady who'd called him a worm, a very nervous young lady it's true, maybe when she was at home she studied her navel just like he did, now that he lived naked… Maybe she also counted her toes, individual entities if ever there were any.

While fishing he once saw something like the shadow of a cloud. The sky was clear. What giant had glided through the waters?

Leaving his fishing, he went out to the pavement. He gazed at the caps of foam repeating like meringues on a confectioner's sheet. He raised his arms and praised the god of the sea.

Thinking about it, he told himself his mother's God might also allow a god of the sea. A delegate, to express it in trade union terms. Be it what it may, he praised it.

So many things were taken for granted when he lived in West Lanús. So many. Everything, that is.

When the cold comes, water moves to the category of minor things.

Which sea was this he was entering now?

First the fog. Moving across in puffs that made one feel nostalgia for the horizon. It left behind shapes that the wind twirled.

The clouds came down to the water, soup-coloured bellies joined to the sea by the falling snow. Snowflakes, snowflakes.

Then ice covered the whole garden. It shone, reflecting the rusty front of the house in its slope.

Hugged by blankets wrapped around his neck, waist and legs, looking for warmth in the bed, stretching his hands towards the fire of his chairs burning on the pavement, he saw his reserves of water turn to ice. Since tiles were missing after he went up on the roof, it was impossible for him to make a shelter. He lined his body with the Salvation Army magazines and adjusted the blankets above him.

He looked like a chrysalis, waiting in its dark shroud to wake as a butterfly in a neighbour's garden.

When he slept he certainly didn't count on waking up as a butterfly. If you can call that sleeping.

He had stuck his head inside a cover his sister had crocheted for a cushion. His breath gave him the illusion of heat. He saw through the pattern of colours.

The worst began with the ice floes. Animals floated by, frozen like cherries in aspic, watching him from inside the crags that slowly cruised near him, colliding with one another, sometimes with a sound.

He sensed he would not last much longer if nothing changed. The idea of rest seemed appropriate. Even welcome.

He noticed that the water outside now reached up to just beneath the windows. It must be the weight of the ice, he reckoned. The house creaked.

With a noise stranger than any other, the remains of the garden broke off, maybe because of the weight of the ice. The pensioner felt the vertigo of the whirlpools before his feet as the garden sunk, floated up again and between two waters went away rocking, like a flat floe.

From then on the door was separated from the sea by the mere pavement.

Countless screeches disturbed him one day. Nose blue with cold, he abandoned himself to what he believed was his final illusion. He lifted the crochet cover. It was a flight of swallows. They were exhausted. They covered the roof. He went out to look at them.

A blow on his shoulder almost knocked him out. The rusty letters had not held the weight of the birds. 'My Refuge' bounced over the pavement, could be read one last time between two waves, then disappeared.

The pain, the hanging arm almost dragged him to the bathroom. Something in his shoulder had broken. The clavicle? He knew little about this. He tied his shoulder in strips of pyjama.

The swallows had followed him in. Screeching with relief, eyes closed with pleasure, they settled on the wardrobe, on the headboard, in the kitchen.

Only one fish was left. Holding the knife with his left hand, he minced two fillets and placed them on a newspaper. The swallows jumped on it.

He melted ice. They drank.

'Eat. Drink,' he told them. 'You are the owners of the house now.'

It brought him joy to see their feathers, their beaks, their little eyes. To save them the unpleasantness of travelling with a corpse, he went outside to die on the pavement.

A wall like a cliff seemed to block the light. A ship next to his house. A battleship with no windows.

Rather, it had windows. A row of portholes as high up as the third floor of a building.

Well, he said. If they want to find me they will.

Standing up, he had no more chairs. Stroking his beard, he contemplated the panorama. The ice floes drifted away in flocks. The water had turned light blue. His arm in a sling was numb.

When the swallows woke up, one group fluttered around the house with pirouettes of happiness, went back in again and busied themselves pecking at what was left of the food in the kitchen and in the pots.

The pensioner lifted his eyes to the wall. It irritated him to see it there. Why didn't it go away? He remembered the flowerpots where he kept the pebbles. He took aim at one of the portholes. At that height, with his left arm and in such pain, impossible.

He got carried away. The pebbles, white as popcorn, bounced off the metal and fell in the water or on the roof of his house. He forgot his concern about the glass in his windows. He squinted. His aim improved.

He laughed. He remembered a day in his early years when, helped by his father, he hit the bull's eye at an amusement park.

Bull's eye. He had hit the centre of a porthole. It was a special noise.

A face appeared.

*

He returned. He did not look back at the house handed over to the passing swallows.

He slept. For hours. He opened his eyes, changed his position, closed his eyes again. They brought him a plate of soup and a spoon. The soup was black, the spoon heavy. Steam would get into his nose. The soup would get down. He worked on his reconstruction.

Wrapped in his beard, he dreamt. Sometimes he dreamt that his house creaked in the ice. Sometimes that his garden brimmed over with gardenias and daisies, and that a neighbour was coming to make him sign a petition addressed to the mayor. Sometimes that the rocking rolled him from door to table.

Then he would open his eyes and notice the sea was moving more than usual. But he was in a cabin with a small lamp in one corner. He closed his eyes again. He went back to sleep.

Later on, curled up on the deck, he looked at the stars. Once he made out the Southern Cross. He cried.

One day he saw the city of Buenos Aires, wrapped in fog. Chimneys as tall as young girls scattered their smoke messages zigzagging into the fog. A smell of putrefaction, and the city with lit-up buildings was waking, coated in shades of pink.

Of course he cried.

From the dock to Constitución he went on foot. He didn't have a cent.

As for the return by train, it goes without saying: he upset the passengers with his appearance and smell.

There was no water in his street once again.

There was his house; or rather, the plot where it once stood. Nettles. Very tidy-looking neighbours shut the door on his beard.

The Protestant instead shared with him his potatoes and his tin of sardines. He only ate the potatoes. Issues of the magazine were lined up on the table.

'I'm in charge of the humour section,' the neighbour said.

A torrent of tears flooded the face and beard he had in front of him. He had never seen a face so strange, with wrinkles like those.

He found the pensioner a job in the dining rooms of the Salvation Army. There he had his daily bowl of soup. He still does.

THE MAN ON
THE ARAUCARIA

A MAN SPENT TWENTY YEARS making himself a pair of wings. In 1924 he used them for the first time, at dawn. His main concern was the police. The wings worked, with a rather slow swaying. They wouldn't raise him higher than twelve metres, the height of an araucaria tree in San Martín Square.

The man left his wife and his children to spend more time on the tree. He was an employee at an insurance company. He went to live in a guesthouse. Every midnight he put sewing machine oil on his wings and went to the square. He carried them in a cello case.

He had a quite comfortable nest on the tree. It even had cushions.

At night, life in the square is extraordinarily complex, but he never bothered to look into it. He had enough with the foliage, the dark houses, and most of all the stars. Nights with a moon were the best.

Our misfortune is not accepting limits. He decided to spend an entire day in the nest. It happened on a company holiday.

The sun came out. There's nothing like sunrise in the treetops. A flock of birds passed very high over the city far below. He watched them in tears, with a kind of vertigo.

That's what he had dreamt of for the twenty years he had spent making his wings. Not of an araucaria.

He blessed them. His heart flew away after them.

A servant opened the shutters of the house of a sleepless old woman. She saw the man in his nest. The old woman called the police and the firefighters.

With loudspeakers, with ladders, they surrounded him.

It took him a while to notice it. He put on the wings. He stood up.

Cars braked. People assembled. Windows opened. He saw his children in their school smocks. His wife with the grocery bag. The servant and the old woman clinging to each other.

The wings worked, slowly. He grazed the branches.

But he lost height. He came down to the monument. He jumped. He sat astride the hindquarters of the horse. He took general San Martín by the waist. He smiled.

A policeman fired a shot.

One shoe remained hooked on the horse.

But he could fly away. Slowly, he advanced, slightly higher than the heads of those in the square, and no one breathed, observing him.

He arrived at the Torre de los Ingleses. The wind helped him towards the south.

He lives amongst the chimneys of a factory. He's old and eats chocolate.

A SECRET

THERE WAS A YOUNG LADY who had a spare head. She lived in Comodoro Rivadavia. Maybe because of the constant wind, or the monotony of limited society, she began to long for variety.

The first step, as we said, was a replacement head. Since she had Armenian features, she chose blonde.

Every fondness either grows or dies. In both cases it ceases to be a fondness. With her it grew into a need.

She therefore added a few pairs of eyes and mouths, as well as two magnificent breasts to alternate with her own and a set of feet that couldn't have been more graceful.

There are secrets that force a change of scenery. She decided to move to another city. She packed her bags and went straight to Buenos Aires.

For some it was a demotion: from teacher to store employee. According to her, it was a piece of luck.

She joined Harrods, in the children's shoes section. She was happy when she was transferred to perfumes, because patience was not her strong point. Also, she had a knack for perfumes. She sold well, and commissions increased her salary. Which would suit anybody, and her even more so.

Her life was fascinating. She even got to the point of accepting invitations from the same man, an employee in household goods, making him believe she was two women. That is, her, the vivacious Armenian, and a blonde friend living in her house. They went out dancing, and the man, though happy with the liberties allowed by the blonde, ended up proposing to the brunette.

The interest of her life was not limited to such dangers. It took as little as going shopping. Buying shoes for certain feet, bras for certain breast sizes, make-up for eyes and mouths.

Her life consisted of putting things on and taking them off, matching, laughing.

They say love is a trial by fire. The trial came. And it was love for real.

He was a man of the sort they don't make any more. She confessed everything. About the man from household goods. And most of all her secret. It wasn't easy! But she did it. Crying as if her soul were being pulled out, she showed him her collection. She swore she would stay a brunette, Armenian, with small breasts and big feet.

He… went pale, obviously. Leaning out the window he smoked a whole cigarette in silence. Waiting for a word, already regretting her confession, she planned to pack her bags and flee early in the morning to Mendoza. But turning around slowly, he embraced her. He would always love her. No matter what form she wanted to take. She just had to let him know beforehand. Mostly at the beginning.

The happiness of love, when it gives more than is expected. Out of gratitude and joy, she danced a crazy dance, covered him with kisses, wept buckets. They loved each other with abandon. They went to the cinema.

And they were happy. It has to be said that he grew addicted to her, to put it somehow. She had so much to offer.

On her side, seeing her most secret of secrets accepted was a rivet nothing could loosen.

They say a leopard never changes its spots, and it's true. But this does not include fleeing. There are ways and forms. She kept her need for transmutation under control with small eccentricities that harmed no one and which she didn't need to confess. Eating a gold and black plastic bag of the kind used to wrap purchases at her job, cleaning the floor of the kitchen with hair shampoo, going to a costume party without a costume.

One day they decided to celebrate their happiness with a child.

Conceived it was, and it grew larger and began moving around, as usually happens.

Beside himself with enthusiasm and love, the father did everything today in fashion: paternity classes, couples counselling, endless bothers for both. Among these, he decided to accompany his wife during the delivery.

The boy was born in splendour. But wrapped in the gold and black plastic bag. Harrods Household Goods, it said in beautiful letters. He was a good-looking boy, identical to his father, everyone said.

The father left the delivery room. He left the city. He left the woman – and the child – forever. Love is like that, when it feels betrayed.

That's how a secret is. It wants us alone. Alone.

THE CASE OF MRS RICCI

THE CASE OF MRS RICCI was the most difficult the Pension Fund ever had to face in its branch for independent workers. Some think the problem was bigger for the lady herself. It's true. But such coincidences do exist.

To begin with, she was very punctual. Of a frightening punctuality, if one could say so. First in line, green coat, grey kerchief on her head. Authoritarian. The employees exchanged glances when they saw her on the pavement. She seemed to notice it and looked back at them through the glass. Staring, as they say. As soon as they opened the door she went straight to the counter and held out her hand.

'Don't I know about hands,' the main clerk used to say once the case was finished. 'Pensioners' hands.'

It's true she had worked hard, yes. Cooking and cleaning, according to her latest papers. Whereas in her youth, she had been uninhibited. A chorus girl, for instance. They often find placement as cooks when summer is over, according to that same clerk. The cicada and the ant. Mrs Ricci's fingernails, always varnished bright red, were what made her guess that. Work made them chip in parts, revealing dirt here, patches of bare nail there. The choice not to retouch them revealed, to her mind, an untidy nature; it spoke of a happy youth, too happy a youth.

She wanted to collect. Her eyes fixed on those of that clerk, she demanded. The clerk's teeth started chattering the minute she saw her standing at the front of the line on the pavement. Sweat ran down the inside of her stockings, she said. Her tongue stuck to the roof of her mouth.

Somehow she was told no. That she could not be paid.

She shouted things never heard before at the Pension Fund. Men came out of their offices. The young ladies got upset. And she wouldn't leave. Standing her ground, she watched the rest receive their pay. The head clerk had to request a leave of absence: a nervous breakdown.

For this reason a colleague of hers, later her husband, seized the reins of the affair. He went around the houses of Mrs Ricci's employers. Along with the shady figures, he got to know people he considered eminent. The female trade-union founder, now balding, who raised her voice to assert she had never paid Mrs Ricci's pension contributions. And seemed proud of what she said. An aristocratic gentleman, tall and tanned, a judge according to the information, in bad company when he arrived, by the looks of it. A writer with a full head of long hair, half-naked in a musty room reeking of coffee, who said he had paid Mrs Ricci all the pension contributions he owed, as well as those owed by the trade-union founder, whom he didn't know. He also seemed satisfied by what he said. He got proof of the injustices that creep daily into the Pension Fund. He felt sorry.

He gave this information, the writer said, for the simple reason that it could not harm Mrs Ricci any longer. She had died run over by a bus while going out to buy vegetables for the judge.

Deceased: 7-X-76. It was in the file. Yes, they knew it at the Fund.

A former pupil of the Marist Brothers now involved in apostolic work at the Pension Fund went straight to his parish as soon as he came out of the terrible meeting with the writer.

A pleasant smell of stew filled the office. The parish priest said he would go punctually the next payment day. He didn't need to be told when it was. His own mother was retired. On that day he would be by his side.

It was reassuring to see him looking so sturdy. Even the cluster of warts covering his left eye gave an impression of good sense.

Everyone at the Independent Workers' Pension Fund anxiously awaited payday.

There she was. With the green coat. With the grey kerchief. At the head of the line.

The door was opened, people began to file in, Mrs Ricci came up to the window.

'Stop!' The parish priest's voice was like a cannon-shot.

She looked at him in anger.

He waved his arm at her, bathing her in holy water, which seemed to spill on the floor without touching her coat.

'Lost soul, go on your way! This is not your world any longer!' the priest cried out. Sweat streamed down him.

It was lucky he was there because one of those in line dropped dead. For most of those going to the bank that day, this was a sensitive topic.

Whereas she opened her mouth and exploded in a torrent of abuse. Several employees fainted.

What came next has to do with the tenacity of love and the eagerness of apostolic work. Another look at the file gave an idea to the most entrepreneurial of the clerks. Ah, but how hard it was.

The month passed. The line again. Again Mrs Ricci. Combative as always. She held out her hand. She asked for the money.

'Rebecca,' a small rabbi murmured. Seen from the front, his head looked like a sugar bowl with a beard and a hat.

Mrs Ricci turned around.

'Your parents are waiting for you,' said the rabbi. 'Are you going to abandon them again?'

Mrs Ricci shuddered. She spun around, breathing heavily. Her green coat, her red nails started to disappear, like a vanishing spinning top.

The small rabbi trembled, and a tear rolled down his cheek.

That was the case of Mrs Ricci. May she rest in peace.

IN THE DESERT

SHE

S HE ARRIVED and everything changed. She came on a wagon, eight horses, whips, a cloud of dust! The door opened and it was marvellous just seeing her foot, and the wonderful skirt she shook, and just waiting until she lifted the veil of her hat. Then. First the smile: the sun when it rises. The clear sensitive eyes, the cheeks. The gesture – kind, if you want, conducive to nothing, with which she saw off the tousled men who unloaded the luggage. And they would say goodbye as if they were letting fall a drop of a liquor from heaven that could never be recovered.

But it could. Every year she came back. That patriarch of a brother and her nephews, suddenly gallant, greeted her.

Do you know the story of one of her arrivals from Europe? The men at customs had to wait seven hours for her to wake up, have breakfast, get dressed, come down from the boat. Stomachs empty, shivering by the braziers, they exhausted their insults during the wait. After that, they didn't forget her. They remembered her as an event, a radiance.

Yes, everything changed. The men became gallant, the women shadows. The servants took pride in their tasks: cleaning the floor for her feet was something else. Her tall brother with the ringing spurs would not admit it, but it mattered little.

The following day she would go out with him on horseback. Due to an acquiescent charity, she would not reveal her repulsion for barbarism, her horror of the countryside.

She taught everyone how to dance. One year she brought a gramophone. The house lost its warlike atmosphere.

At long last she could get even. Alone with her favourite niece, her god-daughter, she would open a small suitcase and take out the trinkets that love made her find. She came because of her. They spoke as equals. She would produce a hair tonic brought from Paris, bows, a silver hairbrush, and would change her hairstyle. She took out embroidered camisoles, a tortoiseshell comb, cod liver oil, a doll.

She returned every summer for two weeks.

For her god-daughter's fifteenth birthday, she promised a string of pearls. She described it by letter, on pink paper.

It was 1876.

That year the Ministry of War pushed the frontier two thousand leagues forward. The newspaper said so.

Naturally, there were reprisals. Seven, to be precise, in Buenos Aires alone. Invasions. Namuncurá, Catriel the fratricide, Reumay, Coliqueo, Pincén, Manuel Grande, Tripailao, Ramón Platero. And their armies.

'They left no horses, cattle, houses or people in their path,' said the chronicle.

Or travellers.

PHASES OF THE MOON

FATHER MATÍAS rode three months, and it was his first time. He was a man of faith. That happened in Paraguay. But Paraguay is one thing, this, our pampa, another.

For instance, sleeping on the ground is nothing strange for a missionary. But sleeping on the ground making sure your head points in the direction you're going, since when you wake up there will be nothing to tell you what's north, south, west or east, only the waving of grasses – that's different.

One needs faith to leave Paraguay without complaining, enter the pampa with a few medallions of the Virgin in a pocket, accompanied by a guide with no tongue and feet like leathery claws clinging to a stirrup that is just a knotted strap.

It also isn't pleasant to change horses just like that. A horse is someone you get used to, someone who gets used to you. But to arrive at a human settlement and get permission to leave the tired horse, choose another and free it when you reach your destination because it can return home on its own, is an impediment to the heart's affection. You can't even get used to a horse.

Those were nights of waxing moon. Until the full moon. Despite his fatigue, the priest never fell asleep without admiring the phantasmagoria that filled the world. Born in Germany, arrived by sea, he looked at this sea of grass where fireflies swayed, and preferred not to think what monsters its nights might shelter.

They unsaddled. The guide tied the horses to some bushes, dug a hole with his knife, stuck a bone deep down. He replaced the halters with hobbles so the horses could graze at leisure and even roll about if they felt like it; he tied the hobbles to the bone, filled the hole with earth and stamped it down hard. Then he set about preparing the fire.

The priest took out his breviary and Latin rose from the pages like incense.

He was so worn out by the immensity travelled during the day that those preparations on the ground seemed to smile at him like a little house. The preparations of savages, one might say. An iron kettle started to murmur, a gourd filled with yerba, a lump of meat was pierced by a skewer.

But raise your eyes, priest, and your two homes will vanish. The golden house of Latin and the affectionate house on the ground. To lift his gaze would be a slip into the infinite. When the sun disappears, it leaves us in solitude, which welcomes the arrival of the uncertain.

Midnight. Asleep on the pit where the bone was stuck and which vibrated at the slightest fright of the horses, the guide felt something. The onset of terror prevented him from moving. The priest felt it too. Paralysed, he was unable to pray. The ropes of the horses stretched in a brutal creaking.

But nothing happened; there was nothing nearby. Only whiteness spread over the world.

That's how terror works: it's born somewhere, courses like a thunderbolt, touches someone, is lost.

Daytime was different. Blessed with its birds, no matter what one might say about the strength of the sun around noon.

At the siesta hour, covered in his own sweat and the horses', the priest learned an inn was near. If no obstacles appeared, by early afternoon they could reach it.

Early afternoon, when the colours in the sky deepen. They would get there, leave their horses, sit in a place with walls, see faces, hear words.

The Sapling Inn. A few *ranchos*, a flagstaff in the shape of a sabre whispering in the wind.

'Something's happened,' said the guide.

Too many men, too serious, stood outside the doors.

To the well-honed ear, 'something' and 'crime' are synonyms.

The bald innkeeper appeared. He crossed the ditch

wringing his hands, came up to the priest's stirrup. He spoke in Galician, continued in Spanish. There had been a crime.

In the meantime the guide realised from the row of horses that the meeting had been recent. And something in the men looking at him arrive, their beards and hair moved by the twilight breeze, words left unsaid, brought that midnight terror to mind.

The priest went in. His greeting was answered as if those there – watchful as ferrets – didn't see him.

Instead of worrying over whether he was thirsty or hungry, which was his duty and profession, the innkeeper tried to take him somewhere else. And even the priest understood that this death hadn't been a classic one.

Resigned to be faithful to his profession, he looked for a stole and followed the innkeeper. The guide and a few boys followed.

In the *ranchos*, colts' hides hung like doors allowed glimpses of women's faces: white, Indian and a black one. The innkeeper walked on under a pink-streaked sky crossed by flocks of birds as high up as fleets of angels on their way to paradise.

In the half-light, which reeked of hides, the stock of rhea feathers waved. The dead body lay on the ground covered with a white poncho. White socks and white espadrilles peered out from one end of the poncho; from the other, a beret and a white forehead. It was a Basque, a shepherd, a loner.

The priest put on his stole, then leaned down to uncover him. The priest's memory held dead by the score. In this one, the bad thing was the expression on his face: terror. The worst, the shape of the wound on his throat.

Without knowing what he was doing, he said the prayers of the dead.

They went out. The innkeeper expected a question. He didn't ask. Huge and red-faced, he did not seem needy. But he was. Thirst, sleep, hunger.

Waiting for the meal, he leaned on the counter. An old man was starting on a glass of Hollands. He offered it to him. Not knowing the local customs, he decided to wet his lips with it and give thanks. He got it right.

The old man was dressed in a garment that reminded the priest of a certain violin he had come across in the jungle: something out of place. It was a frock coat. Threadbare and greenish, with buttons from all over, yet still a frock coat. Above it, from behind a beard, the following phrase came out: 'The things you have seen, Father, surely you never believed in them.'

The priest understood that he had seen nothing. And in a loud voice he asked the innkeeper how that poor man had died. The innkeeper went out to look for food.

Father Matías ate, drank, asked to be called before midnight, and fell asleep in the warehouse, between two boxes of soap.

When he was shaken he woke up smiling. He met again with the stink, an oil lamp smoked near the inn-keeper's elbow, bunches of candles hung by the wicks, like cut off heads. A man of faith, he became a priest again.

But this pampa is not like Paraguay. No man seemed interested in the sacrament of confession. They looked somewhere else, they sneaked in through the door. He spoke, he joked, he threatened. He dragged a boy by the arm and forced him to kneel. He confronted the old man in the frock coat, who stuttered drunkenly. He had to be content with the innkeeper and the women, who made him hear things he didn't expect. He distributed among them his supply of medallions of the Virgin.

A nearly perfect moon was emerging. Each one remembered the one waiting under the white poncho, which at midnight would end his first day as a dead man.

In the light of the moon, the flagstaff in the shape of a sabre surprised the priest in an unpleasant way. In the warehouse the Basque was still covered, the women prayed, the men looked on. The black woman took a step forward, flabby and fat, trembling.

'He was good,' she said. 'A good man.'

She pulled the kerchief off her head. Bald and wrinkled surfaces were revealed to the priest.

'Embers,' she shrieked. She pointed to her skull. 'The Indian women. I was a prisoner, I was young, I was beautiful. You can believe it. I served in the house of a president of the Republic; I was born there. You can believe it. Someone has to avenge this man.'

Hammer blows had been sounding for an hour. The door opened. The ostrich feathers swayed. They brought in a coffin made with beverage cases.

Without uncovering him, they lifted the corpse off the ground and put it in the coffin. They nailed the lid over the white poncho. Just like that, with the grimace of terror on his face and covered by drink brands, a man whom everyone said in life had never known fear and was a teetotaller was left for the other world.

The sun appeared over the edge of the sea of grass as the priest said mass on a door set at the foot of the flagstaff.

Seen under the sun, the flagstaff revealed itself to be a bone planted in the middle of the *ranchos*. A rib, from what monster?

The Sapling. A fitting sapling from a landscape without trees, thought the priest; the meeting of paths that converged from everywhere like the trembling legs of a spider.

When a man of faith determines on a course it's no easy thing to intimidate him. A cart went tumbling away with the coffin on top and the priest, considering what he had heard during the confessions, let the guide know there would be a change in his programme. A new path. 'Where there is evil I must bring Good,' he said.

But the guide also had his own faith, and determined his own course.

So when the priest got his head out from under the poncho that had sheltered him during the night, he found himself alone near his horse. Embers, a bundle with the roasted meat, a water bottle, spoke of a last good wish.

As far as the rest went, only grass and rising sun.

He answered with an act of faith: he opened the breviary. Once he'd finished the prayer, he rode in the direction opposite the sun, a new itinerary that went towards the east.

For an entire day he travelled. At sunset he dismounted, tied his horse to his wrist, ate a little, prayed a lot, tried to sleep beneath his poncho. The voices of vermin sounded in the night. When he woke up he found himself without a horse. The halter, wet with dew, was a stump.

He opened his breviary. Then he tied the food to his back, abandoned his riding gear and began walking.

Near sunset he sank his foot in a hole, sprained his ankle, fell on the ground.

He cried. Tears no one dried as he lay lost in the grasses under masses of stars. He bandaged his ankle with a strip of his cassock.

At dawn he heard galloping. He stood up, faint with dizziness. Three riders stopped right before him. The haunches of their horses were covered in jaguar hides, which dripped blood. The men seemed happy despite the fright his appearance gave the mounts.

The way they carried him is no small thing to tell, his foot all purple and swollen. The men were brothers and jaguar hunters. Like a mirage, three more riders joined them. Brothers too, looking the same, just the same. The only difference was that they had the priest's horse and harness with them.

When the fox is hungry, Father, he eats hide. Even more so if the hide is wet with dew.

The priest remembered the dew, the voices of vermin, the cut-off halter.

Then he seemed to see the plain turn into water, and some grazing cows suspended above the water.

It was an optical illusion, but cows and water existed.

Being a missionary can mean finding yourself with a bandaged foot for weeks, sitting on a cow's skull in front of a *rancho*. It can mean watching six young men and six girls laugh and come and go, sturdy, short and dark, and a gaggle of kids who don't call anyone Father or

Mother run about amidst the hens and lambs raised at home, and dogs; and parrots that climb down clumsily from a hoop to fix a watchful eye. The owner of the house almost always accompanied them, sitting on top of another cow skull, drinking maté. Sometimes in the river a boat crossed the horizon and covered up the cows, small as they were.

The missionary wanted to know about those thirteen sons and daughters, the origin of those children sprung from the earth. The girls decorated themselves with bows, and waited for their brothers alongside the cattle gates. He never got any answers.

'This is the one who matters to me,' the mother said.

She caressed the hair of the youngest one, lying down by her side, his body huge and fuzz over his lip, his cheeks bloodless and hands hanging. Standing up, he was as tall as the door where the foal hide waved on windy days.

'He's sick. Cure him for me, Father, if God brought you.'

One of the elders of the family used to slowly drive the milk cows, before dragging his feet to another skull, pulled up against the wall, where he then sat. Toothless, he told stories of battles, pointing to a blunderbuss hanging from a horn. Father Matías didn't understand a word.

'What's going on with you, son?' he asked the younger.

The younger passed a hand over his eyes and smiled like an idiot. A tear fell.

And the brothers arrived with the jaguar hides, laughing, the ponchos wrapped around their arms for the fight now turned to rags. The younger suffered fainting spells when he saw the blood, but none of the others even seemed to see him, ever.

Father Matías, while waiting for his foot to get better, brought together the kids and taught them the catechism. One morning he baptised them all, and they celebrated with a roast. Eating it, he realised that baptism should extend to the youths. They seemed to agree, but the catechism didn't continue. With a joke, or some mumbled reference to a job to complete, they scattered like the wind.

Being a missionary implies not complaining, and complain he did to the lady of the house. He talked about everything happening to him. How could he possibly preach charity to an innkeeper desiccated with greed, chastity to women who survived from the lack of it, pity to men armed with daggers like swords? How could he ask for peace for that death, that Basque crazy with terror? And in that house…

'You are from another land. Everything is different in this land. Who is the Basque that died?'

'Don Juan Echepareborda,' said the youngest. 'Don Juan Echepareborda, amidst the sheep.'

He laughed wildly. His mother took hold of his head and hid it under her apron.

'Cure him for me. None of the rest matters.'

Every morning and every afternoon, the young man massaged the foot of the missionary with stinking fat. The swelling shrank. The missionary looked at the cheeks, the fuzz over the small red lip. He explained the doctrine, but didn't know if the young man was listening. He asked him a question: didn't he want to talk to him about something?

The eyelids of the young man trembled.

Those were dark nights. The moon at the start of the journey had waned and could be seen above the pale blue, far away, absent and distracted amidst the clouds.

The priest slept with the young man, dogs, lambs and parrots. Stretched out on the foal's hide he heard laughter, a boy who cried in his dreams, a bark. He heard the wind. He heard the boy whimper in his sleep. They woke at dawn. He saw the shadow of bags under shifty eyes. He prayed for him, and told himself he had to make him smile.

Dragging his foot, he went to the field behind the *rancho* where *bocha* was being played. The others made him join in. The mother appeared suddenly, watched a while, vanished.

He was a man of the faith. He spoke to the boy of the other world, where peace awaited him. He looped the last medallion in his pocket, which hung from a red thread, over the boy's neck.

One day he saw the hint of a smile, like a bubble that makes its way with great difficulty through the swamp and finds itself in the open air. He understood it as the message of a submerged soul, and had to hide his emotion.

Sitting on the cow skull, he told the mother that the boy was no longer sad. The father of the family, who had trimmed the horses' manes while the moon waned, now busied himself with other things as it waxed. The growing of the moon made the mother nervous.

'Cure him for me,' she said. 'Haven't you seen him sleep?'

It was true his nights were worsening. When he got up and walked through the shadows, the animals would nestle up against the priest, trembling.

The moon's rays fell like faint rain through the poorly thatched roof.

The priest was tired of inaction and wanted a good gallop. He thought the exercise would be good for the young man.

'Let's go to the Salado,' he said one afternoon. 'I want to see it flow.'

The mother brought them the horses. She seemed tormented, and clung to the stirrup.

'You know what he does. You know what he does. Isn't it true? You know what he does.'

'Yes,' said the priest.

As with the case of the inn he understood he didn't know anything. But he dug his heels into his horse and the young man dug his heels into the other, and they galloped. At the *rancho* the twelve brothers came out to see them leave, as well as the father of the family and the mother.

The only ones who kept moving were the animals and kids playing.

At sunset they arrived at a stream of yellow water that flowed into the brown river.

They prepared to light a fire and make a few matés. A barge arrived, carrying something like a curved pole.

In it the priest saw a man like himself, bald, red-faced, bespectacled. He ran to the shore, and shouted to him in his native tongue.

Yes, he responded in German. He was a naturalist, and was carrying this bone to a museum.

'Wait for me!' the priest yelled. 'Tomorrow I finish a mission.' He thought of the young men he wanted to baptise. 'Wait for me until tomorrow.'

Joy and relief swept through his soul.

'See you tomorrow!' the other yelled. He gave the name of a place on the coast.

'See you tomorrow!' He repeated the name of the place. 'Tomorrow. Tomorrow. Until tomorrow.'

But another, very hoarse voice called the priest from the rowboat.

Grabbing the bone and waving his shirt tail, the old man in the frock coat stood up.

He pointed to the young man and then at him, Father Matías.

'Beware,' he yelled. 'Didn't I tell you, Father?'

He stretched out an arm with shaking finger. At the edge of water an enormous moon was coming out, red as the sun coming to rest before them on the sea of grass.

The priest also lifted his arm and waved. He said goodbye in his native language, which sounded over the water like a kind of home, much sweeter than Latin from a breviary. He looked at the bone and at the old man in the frock coat moving away. He dried his tears.

He went back to the young man to share his happiness with him. He saw him crouched beside the embers with hands clenched, his teeth chattering. He lowered his eyes, ringed by new shadows, and decided to return.

They returned. As they travelled through the country, whiteness took shape like a thickening liquid. The horses whickered and moved their ears.

The priest grew restive with their unease. He remembered the whiteness of the previous month. He remembered the guide who had abandoned him, and prayed for him. He remembered the dead man. Exactly one month before. He prayed once again for him.

It was almost midnight. The horses trembled and blew out air like the horses of the six brothers when they had carried fresh jaguar skins.

'I can see the light at your house,' he was about to say to the young man.

The terror of that time arrived suddenly. It made the horses rear. The one he was riding flung him down and galloped away.

Fallen, he saw the young man hurtling himself at him, tall as the bears in Germany, foam streaming from his mouth. He heard the howl. As he fought, he knew what the Basque had seen during the previous moon, amidst the sheep. He understood what the necklace of tooth marks was, and the expression of the face under the white poncho.

The fall and his twisted foot stripped him of energy. He pleaded as he struggled, but hands of invincible force ripped out the collar of his cassock, sent buttons flying.

There was a bang. A spurt flowed over the priest from the young man's chest.

He saw the eyes grow opaque, then sweet.

'Baptise me, quick.'

He did, with the blood he collected in his hand. He saw the smile that had been waiting so long. He saw the expression of bliss. He saw the family elder holding the smoking blunderbuss.

He saw, then didn't see. He felt pain and compassion. He died of them, right there.

A CAMALOTE

READING WALTER SCOTT it occurred to me to build a castle facing the Paraná. It made me happy with its battlements, towers, drawbridge. A *camalote* brought a tiger along the river from the northern region.[*]

It killed my wife and three children.

Reading Walter Scott I forgot where I was.

I will not forget it any longer.

[*] *camalote*: a cluster of aquatic plants carried by rivers.

DOMINGO ANTÚNEZ

I PREFER TO SLIT THROATS, though my marksmanship isn't bad. Almost all of us prefer it, but it isn't always a matter of choice. If I've been chosen by fate, at some point I will have to pay for it. Almost no one can match me at following a trail.

So I set out early with a few matés and two horses, the first mine, the better one belonging to someone else. I thought of buying it, along with some other things, with the promised bounty. The saddlebag was ready for the proof: his head.

What I knew about him, to start, was that he was in Indian territory. Why? Because he had enemies everywhere.

I thought I knew everything about the desert, but had to learn the worst: a shout, suddenly silenced. As for the rest, the thirst and cold, nothing was lacking. From what I can recall, that was the worst time.

After a month or so travelling, I came across a fugitive captive. French, he said. Engineer, he cried. I don't know why, but I preferred that he die. I left him there.

In Indian territory I met with such a commotion that no one asked me a thing. The chief had died. With him alive, they had put the government itself in a tight spot. Without him, little hope remained for them. A huge gathering had been arranged for the funeral.

Where could I go where I wouldn't know anyone? The men there found themselves on one side or other of the line out of sheer luck. I greeted one of them.

They pointed him out to me without my asking. He rode at the head of his people; he was blond and wore a black poncho and hat with coloured feathers.

There will never be another funeral like that one. But I only mourned the horse and the silver, which they buried with the dead man and his women.

That night I made the most of the occasion to drink mare's blood. I didn't have to be asked twice.

Passing over to his camp – far-flung tents and even some houses – took me time, weeks. It is said that few were as suspicious-minded as he was.

I behaved myself, and a few months later was put on lookout. The moon appeared late that night, and I got the horses ready, keeping the saddlebags close. The weapons seemed to unsheathe themselves on their own.

While I waited, I spied on him through a chink. I saw him sitting there, three of his women with him, all young. One was a captive about fifteen years old who hadn't been there long. They served him and he ate. He was given water to wash. There were fine ponchos and blankets on the ground.

When he undressed and got up I saw that there had never been a man like him. I looked at him and my life seemed to scroll past before me in its entirety. It seemed hollow.

I couldn't kill him.

I didn't return, I didn't ask for payment. What's worse, I passed for a coward. In this campsite, away from everything, I came to stay.

It was fate.

THE THIRTY-THREE WIVES OF
EMPEROR BLUE STONE

I

BEHIND THE GREAT KING hangs a painted hide. It can shake; it's the wind. Or not: the queen is listening. I count on me those dead by his order. Those dead by his hand are in me. The women who cry for their lost youth are fools: they do not know the secrets of fermentation. Look at the drunken revelries under the stars. If water is for day, alcohol is for control.

Old age is a drunkenness. I've lost my teeth, but influence nourishes me. I plait my white hair. What would be plaited without me?

Yet I have a longing. I'd have that girl killed. And the little boy in her arms.

2

I like to soften hides. Eat. Go to get water. Spin fleece, prepare threads, weave. Look at smoke, see if it will rain tomorrow. Defecate calmly among the shrubs. Season the deer through the wound. Prepare maté and drink it. Dye ostrich feathers.

Each day its own. A good life. Sleep.

3

I make people travel. Rider, beware. Of what we visit nothing can be told. The most terrible of kings moans like a lamb. I have never needed beauty.

I am she who travels. The gateway of journeys.

It's true I take risks; I see death at each step. How can I limit to just one this body of mine, of a thousand lives?

No one is as young or as old as I am.

4

I tortured them. I remain thirsty. I saw them die, naming unknown people in other tongues. I was not satisfied. Even if each blade of grass could be subject to shame and each star were an eye to blind, my yearning would persist.

5

Woollen, woollen is the morning. Shoos out the dew, kills off the chill. Red it dyes, warms the eyes. It ties the paths of life. Black, a knot, white, across. Form is pattern, pattern is my form. Here, the line of silence, the fringe, madness, the rake of the sun, the peaks of the night, treads, traces, footprints. Life is among these steps: the yes, the no, the now, the never.

This is the poncho I wove for the king.

6

Friend, give me your mouth. Open your legs for me. I picked fleas from your hair. Fat ones for you, middling for me, thin ones to die between the fingernails. Something happened. It matters little to me to be the king's wife. It matters little to you to be the king's wife. Is it possible to hide it? There are so many eyes.

7

I won't speak of another time, another tongue, another man, other children.

Here, the wind, the horror.

Rocking, sleeping, I am the oven and the bread. Nine batches. Nine loaves of bread.

I see six with the horse trainer. One, with the *bolas*. One, with the lance. One, with the dagger. One, with the hobbled gallop. One, with the footrace. One, lying down.

They will speak amongst themselves, I will be a single ear: horses, horses. Only horses. Can other words matter to me? Can they matter?

There are two more: they run close to my steps. What steps do I hear but those?

There is one more, and he sleeps. Happy bosom. I once had a garden. No petals but these eyes exist now.

Nine loaves of bread. They will go, in this same wind, to kill other children.

8

To go, without footsteps. Ants. Air. Nothing.

9

I glory in his glory.
I repeat, so the wind carries it:
Two thousand five hundred leagues of confederation.
Two thousand lancers.
Four horses for each lancer.
This is how a king's grandeur is counted
I walk, heavy with grandeur.
Why did he mount me only once?

10

The marquis murmured: The chaise is tied. Madam, all that remains is to flee. She raised her mask. Her light blue pupils were goodbye. She slipped a ring with a seal into his hands.

I can't remember how it went on…

11

I will forever see him as ridiculous. Every night watching over his females. He found me with my friend. He sunk in my face with his *bolas*. Then he went to sleep. In the morning he called in my companion. He asked for twenty sheep.

I remained blind.

Twenty sheep.

In the land of shadow I continue to see him. Ridiculous.

12

My grandmother – such a long time ago, on the other side of the great mountain – had an ear for the dead. Walking through the fields she said:

'Here, people are buried. Dig and you will see.'

We dug. The bones appeared.

With the years that sense of hearing was opened to me.

Others, from the taste of the wind, know where the enemy is. I have dealings with the dead.

While looking for a herb to dye the wool I often go walking. At some point the dead call.

They call out, like a warrior in the drunkenness of sleep, like small children in the night. Their yellow bones are already dust. I tell them to sleep.

'We walk during the day. Soon night will come.'

13

There everything was glory. With my cousin I raced horses. We tamed them. Mine braked without reins. It didn't stop to drink, it knew how to wait. We had an example, the most beautiful: Nahuel, a horse of my father's. We were barely more than children.

One night I heard the witch sing, like the water in the cooking pot. She was speaking with the devil. The smoke from her fire responded.

'What frightened you, lord?'

'I will tell you, I will tell you.'

'What drew you away?'

'I will tell you.'

'Come back to me, I'm an orphan. I can't fly any more.'

'What frightens me is the creature that eats from the chief's hand. Its neigh frightens me, its smell scares me, its mane suffocates me. Its feet break my strength. Each blade of grass it swallows chokes me.'

'Do not fear, lord, you will return. It will die.'

I crawled and woke my cousin. I told him. Nahuel, my father's horse, heard us. He did a turn around his peg. My cousin talked in my ear: 'Go to sleep.' I didn't sleep. Hardly more than a boy, he slit the witch's throat. Dawn found her face to the fire, burned to the bone.

There was a shout in the morning. We played with our horses.

What a meeting, what talk, what raised arms, the children hid, the women sharpened their nails. My father put on his cloak, the crown of wool.

'Dead she is,' he said. 'And dead she will remain.'

Much was spoken in low voices, not in front of him. Who killed her, how was it that no one was being punished? Not even my father knew. But a great prosperity came.

What did it come for?

The king of kings – but king among kings – asked for me in marriage.

I asked my cousin, 'What have we trained our horses for, if not for this?'

And we escaped.

My father mounted Nahuel. Nahuel caught up with us. My father carried his spear. He lifted it and shouted.

'It's true I love you like a son. It's true you were going to be chief.'

He killed my cousin. He shut himself away in his tent. He drank for three days. On the third I said, 'Your prosperity was due to the one that you killed. Nahuel witnessed what happened. Your prosperity attracted the king of kings. Now he will leave you, you will see.'

Covered in silver, I was brought to the old man of the blue stone.

Now Nahuel has died, my father is a beggar, and his scattered tribe gnaws on rubbish.

14

He was born. I always dreaded it: blue eyes. The king, my cousin and an uncle came to see him. The wives concealed their pleasure. I expected death. He smiled.

'Good blood,' he said. 'He will be king.'

15

May he die, defeated. May he, foot on the ground, see himself fettered by chiefless soldiers. May his sons betray him, and he know it. May he lose his manly force.

May he die. And his race be erased from the earth. Myself along with it.

Cursing him.

16

My father found me trying to fly. I have never understood the tastes of men. Less so, those of women. Lives of shadows.

Now I know. I look for snake eggs. Toads. Sleeping bats.

The sorceress receives my adulation.

I will learn.

17

A traveller saw me: hopeless, moribund, very beautiful.

It was a mistake. I never existed at all.

Outside I can hear the birds sing.

18

I am two. I have two names and I am two. One morning I lost my first tooth. My mother – who cried all the time – said, 'María of the Angels, bury it, so a miracle sprouts.'

I buried it near the tent. The next day I went to look for the miracle. I didn't see anything. I sat down and waited. When I returned, my mother – you could count her bones – had died. Clubbed to death. It seemed to me she was smiling.

No one else called me María of the Angels. Only I said that. No one said miracle.

When I buried my eighth tooth I shouted in the middle of the field, 'Miracles: I won't wait any longer! I will forget the name María of the Angels! I will just be White Cloud.'

That night, asleep, I heard a song. It said things I had never heard:

> Boat on the sea, rowed ever so softly
> Castle on the river, take away the shiver
> Snow on the hill, it stays with me still
> Angels and saints, go sing your plaints

I asked one, an interpreter with a red beard: what is boat, what is river, what is rowing? What castle, what snow, what hill? He told me, and I repeated his answers to myself while collecting wood and fetching water.

One day an old man came to us.

'The king of kings living on the other side of the desert gives notice of what he has learned from the man of the red beard. A white, fat, blonde child lives here.

He is sending for her. He will deliver many cattle, many horse blankets, a great deal of silver.'

'What child is that?' I asked.

They poured riches on me. We were poor. That king didn't know our village, or our chief.

Now I am a wife, far away from there. I have two names and I am two.

When I find my mother she will tell me why.

19

The pleasure that remains to me is to contemplate the dew.

The dew on the bushes. The favourite queen making her debut with her child in her arms. She laughs. The king wants her close.

On the spiderweb are beads of dew.

In the afternoon I shut myself away, I light a fire.

In the afternoon there is no dew on the bushes. The web is heavy with insects. The dust clouds on the horizon fly.

20

Sometimes I cross paths with the king. If he feels like it he greets me and goes on. Youth, I do not know where it went.

We have been accomplices.

He is not lacking for anything. In triumph, punishment, killing, glory, luxury.

But only I have seen his tears.

2 1

I gave myself up to mystery.
What was it?
A path of darkness
to a land that perhaps does not exist.
I am faithful. I persevere.

2 2

This happened when we crossed the big mountain. While playing, my brother and I climbed up to where the ice is very quiet.

In a cave a girl was sleeping.

Gold on her crowns and on her chest. Her sandals were of green beads, and she wore a mask of pearls. She slept.

When we descended he died of cold. I lived.

We never said a thing.

They call me wife of a king. I wear a silver necklace.

No one knows about kings until he has seen the princess asleep in the mountain.

23

I waited ten years. Then he saw me.

He came from the war. Black blood ran down his chest. I saw his children, his grandchildren. The feathers on his spears, black also, mad with victory. Women, old men, dogs, children were one single howl. And the captive women were the colour of death.

I kept my gaze fixed on him. He reined in his horse right by my feet. I didn't budge. My grandmother slapped me.

They celebrated for many days. The warriors slept, vomited. I waited. The king walked among the tents. I saw him open the leather flap of my house.

I never named him. He never named me. I was king, he a girl. I learned to rule, he to laugh.

People talk often. They know little of love.

24

The moon has a halo: kings are travelling.
My brothers arrived.
The rain erased all the signs. I wept.
My brothers left.

25

The story, which still makes people talk, actually happened this way.

My female cousin had a favourite dog, used to nipping heels. I saw that young man had his heel wounded.

I got hold of some poison seeds and kept them in my hand.

While dyeing wool with the old queen, I cried. She promised me a necklace of beads if I said why. A necklace of beads.

I said: 'My cousin and her sisters are preparing a poison. That young man brought them the seed. They want to kill the king.'

I showed them my hand.

My cousin, her sisters and that young man were burned alive.

They have been dust and ash for seven years now. I wear the bead collar.

That fire keeps me awake.

I asked for his love and he made fun of me. And was he visiting my cousin at night?

26 and 27

We are sisters and different. The day of that double feast – that bloodbath – we worked together. Without warning, the small chief and his two hundred men arrived to visit. They were having lunch and his brothers arrived, four hundred lancers in the dust. Another feast.

They gorged themselves both times.

The king in person passed through the rows of those eating and drinking. He spoke and laughed.

I can assure you: it was a proud day. To be the wife of a king, to feed six hundred and laugh.

But my sister said, 'I know the salt from the kitchen of those kings. Tears and sweat. Sorrow and weariness.'

28

While preparing the king's pipe I have heard how he dictates his letters. The men who serve him make lines and dots, the way white men do.

In the afternoons I sit. I am old. Words don't interest me.

I see birds. Lines and dots. Each afternoon the same letter written in the sky.

Always the same one, which I can't say:

Defeat, end.

29

My brother, lord of the country of apple trees, wanted an alliance with the great one. He pledged me as a wife. When I arrived he was hunting ostriches. He returned at night and left for war. Afterwards he wanted to see me.

He didn't like me.

He went through the ceremony because of the alliance with the lord of the apple trees.

He never touched me.

I had no friends.

The witch asked me a favour: I listen to all the conversations for her, I spy on every tent.

I have been given nicknames. The kids lay traps at my feet. I receive a blow from a piece of rubble thrown at me.

And yet my mother used to tell me stories, she promised me happiness.

30

I dreamt: I lost a tooth.

What will I do without him, what will he do
    without me?

Wind has risen over the river.

What will he do without me, what will I do
    without him?

3 1

It was raining. And my face rained with tears. I felt sad to be the wife of an old king. It was night, under the blanket. Things are like this in autumn.

My daughter's husband entered in the darkness. He'd been drinking. Maybe it was a mistake.

That was like coming into the light on a battlehorse. It was running. It was winning.

3 2

His father told him the day of the first combat:
'Never let a woman matter to you more than war.'
His father told him the day of the first feast:
'No woman carries you further than alcohol.'
His father told him the day of the first sacrifice:
'To tie yourself to a woman is to distance yourself
    from the mystery.'
He got to know combat, alcohol, mystery. He told me:
    'They are three shadows next to your red skirt.'

3 3

I have seen a vision that is not a lie in the water of the well. I saw the king's funeral. It won't be long from now.

His horse will go with him, covered in silver. His wives will stand in a row, waiting for their skulls to be broken. His favourite in the red dress will have the boy in her arms. He will be snatched from her at the same time she is killed. This is how I saw the funeral, with thirty-two wives. I escape tonight.

IN THE GARDEN

THE RATS

WHEN THE HOUSES were knocked down to make the 9 de Julio Avenue, thousands of rats had to look for a new life. They'd had years to prepare themselves. Between the construction of the centre of the avenue with its obelisk and the addition of the two ends, more than half a century passed. But no one can prepare for half a century.

One day work resumed.

I won't even try to describe what that demolition was like. Earth piled up to the sky, people swallowed and chewed it. The first to fall were the ledges with their weeds. The rats fled.

There were too many scenes of desperation to count. Great suffering.

The afternoon a wet rat entered through the ventilation pipe of a tea house on Cerrito Street is just one case of many. A European lady – here on account of the war – threw it out on the pavement with one swipe of the umbrella. But let's imagine: afterwards, on the pavement. Let's imagine: before.

An enormous mother about to give birth entered the beauty salon on Santa Fe Street. The employees yelled and leapt up on the chairs. Thank goodness there were no clients, said the owner, they prefer to get up late. What a search through the dressing rooms, between make-up pots and tiny pink linen pillows. A company closed everything and threw in a lethal smoke. The sofa cover was unstitched. There she was, with all her young, all dead. No one heard about it because the salon owner, a French lady, knew what it was like to earn a living in a foreign country. No one learned about it.

In the north sector there was a male who had never formed a family. He was missing a tooth and was blind in one eye. It was said he couldn't imagine what fear was. If the young admired him, and the old admitted belatedly he was right, the majority looked on him with suspicion. He knew blindfolded the block of hovels and palaces from Paraguay Street to Charcas Street; for months he fed himself in the basement of the Civil Registry. Liberty Square was a trifle for him. He had been through flowerbeds, the branches of the rubber tree and on the cement coverings. On certain evenings, he would climb over the electricity cables at the head of spellbound young ones, moving from tipa tree to tipa tree, from jacaranda to jacaranda. His dashes left a snow of flowers in their wake near the end of spring. He had arrived at the old market on Talcahuano Street where the local army repelled him, earning the bump across his head. That's nothing. He had dared to reach the fair on Córdoba Street with the idea of amusing himself at the dance of the statue. It's a dance around the marble Little Red Riding Hood which until yesterday decorated Lavalle Square. He could see it, just as I did, but it almost cost him his hide since he wanted to join in. People swore he came from the port, where every impertinence meets with applause. Others said he came by train from the silos of Santa Fe. No one attributed his presence to the peaceful procreations which took place in the last decades in the old houses. They may have been right.

One thing was certain. He had ventured to the Other Side at a time before the great rain. The Suipacha Street side. This really makes your hair stand on end.

In the time before the great rain, there were many cats on the flat rooftops around Suipacha. One mother constantly bore young. She spent hours watching the windows of the apartments, because an old man with light blue eyes and his nurse would toss meat down to her from a fourth floor. A kitten of hers fell one Sunday onto the patio of the fur shop. There, Jews with brown fingers cut furs on a table and argued at the top of their lungs. On Saturdays and Sundays the place was deserted. The little cat showed it had good lungs; the whole neighbourhood mobilised to restore peace.

Once in a while the terrible one would slowly cross. It's a cat with an enormous head, also covered in scars. The sight of him paralysed the heart of even the most indifferent.

During the great rain all the rooftops flooded with water; there were weeds like the arms of drowning men on the pale swell. The female cat and her kitten, all grown now, withstood it for weeks with ears furrowed.

Each rooftop was like a pool. One day they were gone.

Those were the regions where the explorer had ventured. They say he once saw the terrible one up close. With cats he had a system; to leap over them, shrieking at their noses. It may well be that he did not know fear. How could he have done all that, otherwise? Just imagine, how? No surprise he was missing a tooth.

In the catastrophe of the demolition many prejudices were left aside. Some rats decided to resort to the one they used to look at askance. Just ask the lady with the umbrella, the owner of the beauty salon, the fur sellers on the patio what kind of tragic compromises are accepted in bad times.

The rats moved forward with an agonising shudder. The hollow houses startled them when knocked down.

Had he talked about a refuge? He had. A temporary but suitable shelter for families with small young. Nearby in which direction? In the worst. Towards Suipacha Street.

For a bitter moment they suspected that the loner was mocking them. The one with no family and no heart was mocking those incapacitated by love. To carry their young towards Suipacha was like offering strings of sweets to the cats.

The explorer was not mocking them. The bad area had undergone changes. Two bars and a Chinese restaurant had opened up. Fat, potbellied, sleepy cats were bred in those depths. They had little to do with the terrible one, the mother, the yellow one, the one-eyed, the champion. He wasn't joking but he didn't give many explanations either. It was a matter of believing or not believing.

They had to believe. They had to go out, trembling, the rosy young in a line, clinging to the rubble, curling up, bellies beating against the ground. If there were any dead? There were. Entire families. The explorer had anticipated it. Beneath the cars green eyes lay in wait. The news of the exodus had spread. Horror once again, shrieks and devastation. It was a question of believing or not believing.

He led them onward. They ran, pressing themselves against the wall. A bark was heard, and they rushed into a pile of boards. Shadows and anguish. They were entering. They had arrived.

But it was difficult. Goodbye hallways, basements, ledges of abundance, galleries of freedom. Goodbye calm. The noises of the day meant sleep was hardly a rest. The men yelled, hammered away, and there was a saw that seemed like the voice of the end. When the sun set, silence arrived. The builders got dressed and left. The night watchman entered his cabin, lit a water heater and sat down to drink maté. He shared his food with the dog. It was important because the dog ate well, so he slept well too.

Meanwhile the demolition progressed. Blocks of houses turned into dunes of rubble. The dunes went away in trucks. Zones of yellow dust remained, lifted into the sky when there was wind. And doors, shutters, windows and balcony railings were put up for sale.

In the neighbourhood, the presence of rats that had fled from the old houses was noticed all of a sudden. After some time it was more than noticed.

They had multiplied. No one could avoid it, them least of all. The building had been constructed slowly, and gave them time to get comfortable. They flourished. They lost the evasive air of the first days. They got organised. They began to consider their hours of leisure, exercise, hunting as a right. They didn't realise there were too many of them.

But they were too many. At night they ran through the scaffolding, they chased one another through the half-built stairs, where light bulbs stained with whitewash shone. They had taken the habit of exploring the walls of the neighbouring buildings, and little by little got used to stopping on the windowsills of the first, second, fourth, eighth floor, of climbing up the telephone cables. Their shrieks were heard suddenly on a ledge. There were people who never opened their blinds again. There were some who regretted not fixing a broken glass in time.

Stories began to circulate. Christmas Eve, the young mother leaves the table set. When she comes back from midnight mass she finds the tree fallen, jasmines strewn about, the turkey nibbled away. Isn't this called making oneself hated?

The great hatred against the rats crystallised. It was time for New Year to arrive. You can't also think about rats during New Year's celebrations. Windows, blinds get opened. Sometimes the river decides to send the city a breeze that lets it sleep. Those not resigned to losing it slept with the window open.

The rats took over the houses. They settled behind the cupboards and underneath the stoves. Everything was food for them. Even the television cables, even the drainage pipes of the washing machine.

Then the war began.

The sale of poisons rose overnight. The garbage men protested since no one likes to find a corpse in the trash can, even less so if it's a rat. The grocer on Juncal Street preferred to buy a cat. You must have seen it watch the passing cars, sweeping the pavement with its prey's tail. The owners of fat cats stopped feeding them.

People started looking in the telephone directories for the address of the municipal offices named anti-rodent, as if otters and hares also figured in their plans. The poorest went early or in the evening, the richest sent their maids. Lines were so long that bureaucratic procedures seemed to dissolve. But the claimants looked at one another with relief, like someone who discovers there are other people sick with the same embarrassing illness. And they talked about the rats. They talked against the rats.

The battle was in close order formation. Traps, poison, gas, cats, even ferrets. The houses transformed into ambushes, the streets into extermination camps.

The rats felt cornered.

Here begins what I am going to tell. They say it started on the floor where they once forgot to replace a kitchen window. The young mother with the young father and children went for a change of air to the seaside. The mother-in-law stayed behind, with her grey-hair bun. The neighbours saw her go to mass at six o' clock with shawl and missal. Someone noticed she was walking in a strange way, as if holding back a hurry, a trot. When summer was over someone asked about the young people's return, and received a surprising reply. No matter which reply. But when he leaned forward to listen to it, he thought he noticed something like whiskers, the bun like a coiled grey tail under the shawl.

The newspaper vendor also changed. He seemed to grow thinner, he started wearing a beret, and instead of yelling out the news preferred to wait for clients, hiding his face behind a magazine.

The doorman of the new building was next. At night he seemed to come out calmly, but in the day, how many buzzes were needed to make him appear, trembling, tiny red eyes, on the verge of escaping? Let's not even talk about the grocery boy. It was, as they say, overnight. He made himself a hat from a rag and started to wear an enormous apron. He didn't get angry at the taunts. 'One must take care of clothes,' he laughed, in a slightly high-pitched voice.

One of the priests of the church of Las Victorias took to spending the day holed up in the confessional. They say that, forced to give a sermon, he had a kind of tantrum and was never seen again.

The warden of Liberty Square was glimpsed early one morning by a group of boys coming back from a dance. He ran around the statue of Don Adolfo Alsina giving shrieks of pleasure.

The neighbourhood changed.

Go down to the grocery store to buy a hundred grams of ham. You have to wait. Suddenly, wearing a dress of light-blue silk and a small hat – look at her, leaning over her wallet. She is old. The cat looks at her. She hurries up, grabs her purchase, leaves brushing the walls.

Pay attention, it's Sunday. The car is shining. The father comes out, the children come out, the mother comes out. They emerge in a line, as if remembering dangers. Wearing suits that are too new. Carrying food parcels. Impatient, not looking at anyone. Come on, this car, get started, get started, there they go.

They still prefer to be in a group; that's natural. Some get together at the tea house at around five o'clock, others come out of the church, others have learned to play bridge. Many are mad about cinema. They go to non-stop features and see the same story five times. Others, calmer, nibble on a newspaper while seated on a bench in the square. There are even some who start talking about pension rights.

They still look a bit dodgy as they go about, a bit sullen. But all will be fixed.

It will be fixed. It's a question of habit.

PERPLEXITIES

As far as family goes, she was both lucky and unlucky. She came from a line of hunting dogs. She heard talks about great feats. That zeal, those souls. All so excessive.

The first illusion was that: family. The second was her beauty. Nobody thought her less than magnificent.

And she was futile.

She felt at ease with the dogs and bitches of the inner garden. The most banal. Surrounded by such feeble personalities, something like the sounding of a remote battalion began to call her. The kind heard among the hunters in her family. And she seemed, she felt, superior to the commoners.

She returned to her own kind, to the outer garden. The call that pounded in their blood now seemed in poor taste. Foreign. She cried when she was alone. She believed herself a dethroned queen.

Maybe she was just weak. Like so many.

BUT ON THE ISLAND!

A CAT ESCAPED from a house full of ornaments. He spent his first few days under a car. At night, hunger and passion made him go out. He avoided fights, ate little, felt weak. When the car left he had to look for another hiding place.

Embarrassed, he found himself eating the meat an old lady brought him wrapped in paper. Until she heard the mocking of a female cat watching him from a tree.

She taught him more than any other in the world. She wasn't young, or pretty. But she was graceful. They spent the days walking through an endless park. Trees of all species, some so big one couldn't even imagine climbing them.

His first hunt was a wounded dove crossing the street, fluttering its wings. The blow and the blood made him understand. He ate everything, even the feathers.

Afterwards he learned how to slink through the branches, take nests by surprise, even hunt rats. That's not to say he wasn't comfortable visiting garbage cans.

One night they entered the zoological garden. He'd never imagined anything like this. He looked into cage after cage, keeping out of reach of beaks and claws. The eagles. The monkeys. He walked along the foul smelling shore where seals slept.

One night he arrived at the lion pit.

Sparse grass covered the hill where families slept.

All else ended for him. He lived for the lions.

Sometimes he arrived later, sometimes earlier. But he never missed the words of the patriarch.

Born free, with scars around his nose, the patriarch spoke every night.

And every night his family members climbed, roaring sideways, towards the tree. The males with manes that fluttered like grasslands. The females put their pups to sleep before going out. They lay down one after the other, the young in the last row.

The cat waited. His hair stood on end. A shadow would have been enough to make him shriek.

In that tongue, words burned, bonfires on a black field.

He didn't understand. They were coups. Places. Laws. Lions that left memories to be handed down from lion to lion as long as the species lives on, free or unhappy. Sands, naps. Watches. Tastes, blood, smoking blood. Leaps, from bushes. Battles. Defeats. Loves. She-lion heroines. Massacred pups. Revenges. The cat felt as if the strange water of a river filled with fish he could not catch was running by him. He dreamt of those fishes, those words. One day he woke up knowing the language.

The patriarch fell silent. A muffled thunder of roars followed. The sheer fact of being lions passed from soul to soul those nights. Tails whipped flanks.

Afterwards there followed days of sun, burning dreams. And blue nights walking down the path to drink from the river.

'Don't let them steal away your brains,' said the she-cat. 'Those are things that lead to death.'

The cat was young. He said, 'I wouldn't mind dying for them.'

One afternoon, he arrived at the zoo at feeding time. He felt the same shame as when dealing with the old lady's paper-wrapped meat, but much more of it.

His constant watching made him notice a young lion, so young there were still vestiges of spots on his fur. In a certain way, he behaved like the cat: he did not live for himself.

He lived for the patriarch.

He stood at his request, even when slumbering, even answering to the lift of an eyelid. He carried the best morsels to the tree, leaving them at a respectful, but not uncomfortable, distance. He arrived at the meetings beforehand. So, while the youth hung on to the old, the cat hung on to the youth.

And he got to know his thoughts better than anybody else but the youth's mother, who watched her son while feeding a new suckling pup.

He also got to know the youth's real name. A keeper called him Juan, and he answered when he was called, and allowed his back and nape to be caressed. But his name was another. He heard it in that language he had just understood.

The cat had got in the habit of spending hours on the tree with a lacerated trunk which threw a fragile shadow on the patriarch. The stench of the gathered beasts intoxicated him. The stench of the souls drove him crazy.

One night he saw the young lion climb the hill. It was early. He heard it stutter. He told his ancestor that he had understood his lessons; this was no life for a lion. He asked his permission, and at the same time announced that at the first chance he'd look for a way to know that thing without which there is no lion. Freedom.

The elder's pain rose like a vapour, and made the cat reel on his branch. He closed his eyes, as if boredom or light disturbed him. Those among us who wish to know such things pay with the end of everything. With death.

The young lion said the same thing the cat had a month before: 'I wouldn't mind dying for such a thing.'

The elder lowered his head. He licked his paws a long time. He said: 'I understand.'

When the young lion came back down the hill, his mother shook the pups from her flank. She rose. 'What are you up to, son?'

'Nothing, Mother, nothing.'

The cat! He gave himself up to the young lion's cause. It was hard for him to sleep. He studied the gates, the schedule, the method of food distribution.

One Saturday he said to the female cat, 'Monday. Early on Monday morning.' He'd chosen well, since on Sundays, by nightfall, animals and guardians were fed up and tired. All of them awaited Monday, zoo closing, rest.

The female listened to him, crouched. Her eyes turned green like two lamps. She would help him. Anyway, she had already lived too much. (She wasn't going to tell him life without him didn't interest her.)

That night the old lion sang. He sang showing his fangs broken in battles, darkened with time. He sang and the other lions, who had never sung, also sang. They sang and the two cats above them, transfixed by the song, caterwauled until fainting.

The same way a ship emerges over the horizon on a windy day, wrecked but still afloat, and the fluttering of its sails gives the impression of life, the life of the lions in the desert rippled through them.

The old lion sang. It was a goodbye to his grandson. His grandson understood.

So did his mother. And the she-cat. No one else.

Early Monday morning, in the drizzle, three men in a car swore they saw a puma and two cats drinking from the monument fountain. Early Monday morning, in the drizzle, a drunk actress said a lioness with her young crossed the avenue before her eyes. (It was a young lion and two cats.)

Drizzle erases footsteps. Drizzle chases away lovers. Drizzle makes scents rise from the earth.

To roll around over the earth, autumn leaves flying between one's claws, sticking wet to the body the colour of autumn leaves. A male and female cat protect themselves, trembling, from humidity. A fire of embers gives off sparks in the drizzle, a female pauper drinks soup under the *ombú*.

Monday at dawn, in the drizzle, a new sailor heads to his barracks. The wind snatches away his cap. He jumps down from the bus to stop it from doing turns in the mud in the park. Hadn't he promised not to do anything worth arrest, to escape notice and get married when he got back? A weight fell on his back, the smell of wild animal, a jet wets his uniform, steams. He is carried away, open-legged; he is broken, savoured, eaten, hot life passing to hot life.

Friends, I don't believe you know a lair comparable to that of the palm trees on the lawn, curved spurts emerging above a tangle of their own species.

A brief sleep for nervous recovery, for digestion. Inside the shelter, the water did not reach them. The cats mumbled.

It was a dream. Adventure called. The young lion left the bushes, lifted his chest. Roared.

He prowled through trees. Strutted. Sniffed. He came to the shores of a lake, and drank. The cats followed, sheltering from the rain as much as possible.

The lion was mad with happiness. He dug into the earth, tossing it up, poking his nose in it, scratching a trunk that gave off bark in strips that were honoured to stop a while in his claws. In the rain, the voices of the night fall silent. They were even stiller that night. But he thought this was normal.

The female cat begged the male to try to make himself understood. But it is one thing to understand a language, another to make oneself understood in it.

The cats believed that day should be spent on an island in the centre of the lake. The bushes touched the water on the shores. There used to be a bridge with lights, which is no longer there. (Friends of the she-cat had been electrocuted there.)

The lion looked at the island. He liked it.

He had to make an effort not to finish off the cats with a swipe of his claw when they returned to speak with him. Growling, he listened.

Cats do not enter lakes, so the lion helped them cross. It would have been easy for them to stay. But they went. They wanted to.

The sun came out and the bamboo shook in the breeze at dawn. The geese on the other island with the stone lighthouse yelled excessively, running to and fro; they had noted the passage of an unknown beast through the water.

But on the island! The sun rose and warmed the earth, bamboo and trees. The heat began to turn the world sultry. There was a magnolia tree in the middle of the island, and, in the magnolia, an incomparable sound. A pod encrusted with red seeds thwacked against the lion's nose. He looked at it, asked the cat if it had made that sound. (The sound had ceased.) No, it had not. It was a thrush, a bird, a morsel who liked those red seeds in the autumn.

On the island! Crawling along paths that led down to the lake. Jumping and playing in the shadows of the leaves. Scratching a tree once again, belly and mouth on the mossy bark. Chasing one's tail in circles until going crazy and tumbling about in happiness, paws in the air. Oh, reaching, stretching, yawning in the breezeless atmosphere.

The female cat said to the male, 'We should have brought his food.'

And to herself: 'The end has begun.'

Climbing to the top of the magnolia, the cats could cast a glance around them.

They saw the avenue with its ever-moving automobiles and buses. The lakes, their rows of boats in the waters. The summit of the monument where they'd drunk water with such euphoria early that morning. The fronds, the trees, known one by one, some hospitable, some not, some fragrant, some not, some secret, some not. The people with dogs and the people with bicycles.

But it was Monday. Few people out. Little noise. The geese themselves were so full from previous days that they rejected the bread someone offered them.

The male cat judged it fit to recommend to the lion he hunt geese that night. The female cat didn't tell him that there would not be a tonight.

Lying on a magnolia branch, one paw hanging down, the lion dreamed. New dreams from new fragrances, of the old lion, of his mother, of his father whose black and enormous mane ran from his chest to his belly. He woke up hungry.

He set off to look for his meal of the previous day.

When he got to the shore he stopped. He peered between the leaves. He noticed something.

All was silent. Not a human being, boat, car or bus. From the summit of the magnolia tree, the female cat murmured something. Twice she had named the male cat with the wrong name, one from the time of her youth. On her palate and tongue she had a feeling, a taste, like the one she'd had that vertiginous night in the trees, when the tabby had died in that manner, when in love with the white one, and she had fled crazed from fear. She didn't care about fleeing now.

A sound broke the silence. The fur of all three stood on end. Something could be heard far off, all worked up. A barking.

The island was circled by white helmets, hands holding elongated objects, dogs tied to leashes choking in the eagerness to hunt, a fleet of boats. Also, certain trucks with lights and cables.

'Juan!' a known voice shouted.

The lion backed away, a gleam in his eyes. Memories of his kin came to him, of food and caresses. And the feeling of cold bars against his nose.

'Juan!'

Night fell.

All the lions surrounded the patriarch. There was no speech that day. By his side were the enormous one with the black mane, and the lioness with her recent young, her milk dry since morning. They breathed against the scarce grass on the hill. They cocked their ears.

A crackling could be heard from afar.

The patriarch flattened his ears and closed his eyes. He was the only one who recognised that sound.

With eyes closed, he saw the young lion fall from a branch, a soft, heavy fall. He saw two small animals riddled with bullets drop onto his back.

The patriarch died just then as well.

A LAWN

AMONG THE GARDENS that run from Palermo to Recoleta there's a square of lawn. One year the gardeners forgot to cut it. The grass grew at its leisure.

Every half-hour a train ran by with rusty breath. The roots felt it pass, the earthworms interrupted their journeys.

The grass kept growing as it pleased.

In autumn, juices went through the earth, just as the needle of a mattress repairman goes through thick wool. The grasses and earthworms were surprised by the novelty.

When the sun set, the doormen of the apartments burned the garbage. Whirlwinds appeared over the buildings. Black papers fluttered around the metal screening of chimney-tops, crumbling in their eagerness to escape. Sparks gave themselves to the air and disappeared; soot rose. The soot from other houses met it. Together, they formed clouds. Broken up by a flight of birds, the passing of a train or a gust of wind, they came to land on the lawn.

The lawn. Near the traffic lights of the avenues, yellow, red or green colours tinted it according to the order of crossing, and over it the cars belched a trail of smoke.

It wasn't really a lawn. It was more of a pasture.

With its soft surface it attracted those in love. Kids too, playing football or toddling about, their parents behind them. Ice cream sellers who when the heat won out came to sit down. And coffee vendors laden with Thermoses, who tried to make themselves heard above the sound of the trains. It attracted the birds, who found good food. And the insects, because it was a forest full of places to shelter.

It attracted the owners of dogs.

The dogs were keen to run, to smell, to do their business.

They had owners of all kinds. The confident ones let go of the leashes. The frightened ones ran behind, tied to them. If women, they twisted the heels of their shoes. Loose and leashed dogs met one another, whimpering; free ones bounded off, chasing each other and returning when they heard their names shouted.

There's an hour of night when those in love have gone home and the trains have stopped, when dew falls on the lawn. The soot trickles down. Each blade of grass retains a dewdrop.

Days of rain come too. Just water, washing, whispering, filling the earth with damp. Not a person, not a dog. Silent, the grass opens its mouth.

One day the city mayor travelled through all the gardens between Palermo to Recoleta. A king had announced his visit.

The gardeners arrived to cut all the grass, north to south, east to west.

And the grass that died sang.

It sang of the breath and rattle of the train, the descending soot, the juices of autumn. The earthworms. The lovers. The traffic lights. The ice cream sellers. The insects. The dogs with and without leashes. The owners of the dogs. The birds. The coffee vendors. The big children and the ones just learning to walk. The dew, the smoke from the cars, the rain.

It sang, that voice of the grass, that smell of freshly mown lawn.

WHITE GLORY

DAPPLE-WHITE HORSES can be bland or they can be the glory of the world. White Glory was the glory of the world.

No glory felt less glorious than he did while climbing aboard the southbound train in the city of Buenos Aires. He came from a confinement almost impossible to suffer. Not so much because of the walls, which he was used to, as because of the floor that constantly slipped beneath him, to say nothing of the lack of exercise. If it hadn't been for Dick taking him out into the fresh air he would have sickened forever. Despite that he kicked down several dividing walls. As soon as he'd left that place he'd had to board a train. His shoulders trembled.

A blanket of dark red with blue trim and four shields covered him. When he reared up, the squares could be seen, blue and green in reverse, along with his straps with gold buckles.

Dick was worse off. He'd suffered in the ship but now suffered more. He didn't want a seat in the train, preferring to sit on a bale of straw with White Glory. The hour came to say goodbye. He had to return to his land. He hadn't prayed since childhood, but now he did, asking to be spared that pain.

If you'd seen White Glory as I saw him that morning in the previous century, with eyes like black diamonds and the head of an archangel, you'd understand Dick. You'd have left your love, family and friends for him, as Dick did. When you saw him, you lost yourself.

Dick carried an envelope in which there was a book of red leather with a blue fillet and gold shields, the blazing list of White Glory's pedigree. Dick didn't understand why the owner had left out the names of those ancestors that trod the clouds and will do so once more at the end of time. They were the most prominent ones, from the Arab side.

The truth is that he'd respected the owner until a certain day, when he learned that he'd traded White Glory for money.

Not only that. He'd sold him to people inhabiting the southern part of the globe. That's where they were now.

That night the train crashed. Dick, who had fallen asleep on the bale of hay, rolled under the legs of the dapple-white horse. His terror was what finally made White Glory lose his head. He cut his halter, kicked down the panels and shot off into the night with Dick's brains stuck to his hooves. He didn't know about the fire that had destroyed the train and turned the book of red leather to ash.

Filled with terror, he galloped into the night. There were burrows in the ground, and he jumped over them without knowing. The night had the strangest smells.

He galloped through grasslands reaching up to his chest. Uneasiness made him turn away from a thicket where an eye gleamed. He galloped without stopping.

Once he was about to rest. But then something whipped him. He'd known the most magnificent riding crops, gold and tortoiseshell, rhinoceros leather. But no one would have dared lift one against him. A nudge of the heel was enough for him to win a race. Now he was being whipped in the dark. He bucked and bellowed, shooting off into the noisy water until it reached his belly. There at last he halted, trembling, his mane dark with sweat. When he stopped, so did the whipping. He saw he was in the middle of a fog as fluffy as Dick's winter scarf. He could smell only wetness.

He drowsed, and lowered his head, but the cold of water against his muzzle made him rear up. Once again he felt whips, and shot off.

If Dick had seen him like that... He was better off where he was, not knowing.

A shadow rose up before White Glory. His mane waved vertically like a very slow bonfire. His back had no end. White Glory's heart beat loudly.

'What is your name?' he heard. Pale edges glowed on

the suspended hooves, a cloud wrapped itself around its endless flanks. White Glory folded his ears flat.

'My name is mine.'

'Is it easy? You think it's easy. It is not easy. It is easy. It seems easy.' He spoke with thunder, and the night seemed to accompany him. White Glory rose up on two legs, clutching at the air, his mane tossing around him like a torrent.

'My name is mine!'

The shadow galloped upward and he lifted his head to watch it. He saw the air rent in tatters as it passed through it. This sky was different from the sky in England, and there were stars.

Dawn arrived. He found himself surrounded by what had seemed feathered riding crops, but was revealed as a forest of sparsely leaved, slender stalks which grew in the water. A mirror-like watery path traced his journey of the previous night. He drank. A couple of little birds fluttered before him, sometimes stopping to land on a stalk.

'Sir, terror, farewell, goodbye, please. Goodbye, please. They are our first ones, we are frightened, we cannot feed them. Sir, please, goodbye, goodbye.'

'Food, food, food, food!' screamed the chicks.

'Goodbye,' nickered White Glory, advancing cautiously through the marshland, hooves smashing snails. There were many nests hanging amidst the stalks. When he emerged from the water a flock of birds that looked like tiny men received him with a racket.

'That's him, that's him, that's him, that's him.'

Then many creatures from the marshland found ways to come look at the Whirlwind of the Night, the one who had kept them in terror for so many hours. Each concealed himself in his own way to observe him, with flights that feigned indifference and silly wingbeats.

That day word began to spread on the pampas of someone arrived for some purpose. A stallion white as a heron with a red back.

The sun came out. Its gaze moved over everything without obstacle, as a billiard ball might roll along a runner, until it hit White Glory's chest, which was as solid as the full moon when it rises over the Río de la Plata. Just like the moon, the chest of White Glory was set aflame with the gaze of the sun almost touching the earth.

The whole world greeted that gaze.

A breeze seemed to lift up to receive it.

Just like when a young officer gallops alongside a returning hero, and the hoofbeats of both horses mingle with one another, for a moment, White Glory thought the gaze of the sun was what bent the grasses, and breeze was what gave light to the world.

He smelled the grasses, and ate without worrying about their toughness.

He was put to the test. Some bad weed, doubtless. His legs gave way. He resisted with a death rattle, dragging himself to the water where he drank all he could. His blanket grew wet at the edges and was soon soaked. After shivering through the night, the sun dried him. Dew seeped into him at dawn. When he fell, he saw a life he hadn't expected: snakes rushing through the grass, ants, the little bird that had spoken to him the previous day dying in the mouth of a horned frog.

Later he stretched out. Legs stiff, belly enormous, mane full of earth, eyes bulging, he listened to the wingbeats of the grey-brown birds and their commentaries, which he didn't understand, but knew referred to him.

He turned dark with sweat. He whinnied softly.

Oh, all the better Dick couldn't see him.

Time passed, a great deal of time. One day he sat up without standing, and the sun seemed good to him.

More time passed, and then he felt hungry. He ate, and how he ate.

The grass brimming with seeds was responsible for his great improvement, his force and splendour.

Over the green plain he went, alone, running just to run, kicking just to kick, until he tired of that place and chose to follow the course of the wind.

He followed that path. When he arrived at a river he saw beings of his species on the other side. Mares. Such a scent. Bellowing, he ran towards and drew back from the water several times. He found a place where he could cross over. It was twilight and when he emerged, he shook off the briny water.

The next day was his first battle.

A black stallion came out of the thicket, sweeping along a tail stiff with caltrop. It came at him, bellowing.

In the depths of his memory White Glory found ways to bite, kick and paw, giving and receiving blows. The two reared up on their two legs screaming, tails arching like banners.

The other horse tripped on his own mane.

He died from that, broken by the blows. He was old and fierce. Dying, he saw the scarlet-caparisoned white one and felt him to be a worthy successor.

All his mares went to White Glory, animals that had no experience of men, girths or bits. From them and for them he learned everything a stud should know. Ponds, grasses, shadows, dangers.

People on horseback, reeking of colt flesh, pursued him in an immense chase. They lit blazing walls of fire.

By then his blanket had fallen apart.

He was the only who got away, for no other ran like him. No one could jump as high or as far. He leapt over the fiery fence. Rumour spread that there was a horse from heaven roaming free.

Yes, he went about free. But once again he was alone. How alone, and how free.

His battle against the pack of starving dogs is spoken about often. He opened a circle with his kicks, then fled, jumping over them and dashing away.

He left behind everything that can be seen. Or even dreamed. He ran until he came up against water. He turned to the south.

Hidden in a stretch of woodland, he watched a multitude of horses advance, their manes so long they reached the ground. As the herd surged forward, he grew agitated, doing turns, whickering, holding back his neighs. He'd learned prudence. He watched, smelt them as they went by. Clouds of dust followed, then nothing.

White Glory's third battle was not forced upon him.

Out of love for a young sorrel he attacked a bay with a black mane, which did not fight to the death but ran away, bleeding. The sorrel and all those belonging to the bay went to White Glory. If Dick could see, how happy he'd be.

He'd have been happy watching him lead his pack to the unassailable region.

Past marshlands, muds, swamps. Leaving deaths. Erasing all traces.

This is how, when the tides of wild horses were extinguished by men, one group persisted. Every generation had a new chief. But they always went south, and were always led by a stallion. White.

It will be a century now.

I've seen them from far off, passing the lake of Urrelavquén. They run over the salty lands, like a cloud. One dapple horse runs in front them all, glorious as glory.

THE RACE OF CHAPADMALAL

Do you know the word Chapadmalal? Literally, it means 'marshy corral'. Its real meaning is a concentration of beauty. A house, a park. And above all, horses.

The best horses go afterwards to the cemetery. There they sleep, and turn into Chapadmalal.

A poet sang of them. No better way of telling the truth.

I only want to remind you that every moonless midnight a race is arranged there. They say only those with a pure soul get to see it.

What they feel is a trembling in the night, a coming and going of hooves. Once again, the fragrance of horse sweat.

Leaving behind the roots in which they are wrapped, the great runners phosphoresce. They go in a whirlwind, a stampede with no stamping, a rush. They wear the afternoon's laurels. The sea isn't far. That much is known.

Oh, to have a pure heart! To be able to see the race of the horses of Chapadmalal!

THAT ONE

O F ALL THE THINGS I was told about that land, that is to say, the space that runs from Gándara to Guerrero, I'd have given anything to see one.

You had to approach in the very early morning, all the better if it was foggy. Then, wait until daybreak. It was terribly damp.

After that the whiteness appeared. The mane on a powerful swanlike neck. The wide chest and bluish muzzle, the virile and fleshless legs. He moved his head, and the mane, like a curtain, fell over one eye, only to rise again and reveal it, shiny as a jewel.

It was the horse that sings.

It sang, yes. Some have said so, those who were lucky. It sang.

And how, with that voice and that sound.

As I said already, I'd give anything to have seen it. Seen and heard it.

But those were other times, different from now.

DAGGERS

BYWORD

THE WORLD IS MY ENEMY.

I started by selling my parents' cutlery. I would have sold their hearts that day.

Things have an unfortunate tendency to escalate from a little to a lot. I wish they went from a lot to even more. That's why I'll leave out the dullness of stolen cars, the races over rooftops and ledges. The dabbling of a rookie is never interesting.

As an ex-law student, I amused myself by winning laughably short sentences. A little jail can't hurt a man, says a tango. Of course not. It won me friendships.

The best, which can never be expressed, came later. There were the groups I led, and my women. The first, the faithful one, went crazy trying to put up with the constant fear.

Every danger will nourish me forever. And I've been nourished…

Border crossings, diamonds. When there was a fuel shortage in Brazil, I flew with tanks of petrol that spilled over the floor. Do you know what it's like to fly on a bomb?

Oh world, enemy of mine.

Now is the hour I've always been waiting for, the true one. Like a hurricane the machine guns, the glass and faces exploding in front of me, leaving a dead partner on each side. The world is my enemy, I'm screaming now, riddled with bullets. Undone, elated at last, serene.

NEMESIS

THE TRUTH IS THAT I didn't cry for my husband. Thirty years of discord. Or rather: ten of discord, and twenty of hate. That's a yoke if there ever was one.

I inherited from him. I had always wanted assets of my own. I invested, bought land – I know how to accept good advice; I took out money in loans.

I became happy, even started to notice colours in the sky.

When I moved into my new house, two rooms with carpets and vases overlooking a park, I drank champagne alone and laughed.

Every Friday I invited friends over for bridge. Old married couples and a pederast to round it out.

One Monday afternoon the servant left. She'd been useless and rheumatic and was going to check into a hospital. A relief.

I asked for help from the doorman, who sent his son.

I don't know how it happened.

I've started to think about stories I never believed. About Cupid, with his arrows and blindfold.

He came in my house and looked at me, and for a minute my tongue didn't respond.

I'd read about that happening in novels, but not to me!

I find myself thinking of more mystical things too, sorcerers and gods. I've grown sick with love.

Ten days ago I would have laughed listening to this story.

He knows what afflicts me, but isn't compassionate. Just the opposite; he hardly conceals his contempt.

He enjoys – like me – money. He builds a little house in a suburb for his girlfriend.

Like me, I said? Trembling, I crawl to his feet, bring my hand to his knees. I give him my money.

I still invite people over for bridge, although now I can't tell the faces of my grandchildren apart. Every afternoon I dress the way I believe I used to, and make visits where I talk about films, politics, fashion.

I return at night, without looking at myself in the mirror of the elevator, burning.

Standing in the kitchen, there he is, indifferent. I run to find him.

What was the world?

RED

'GET THE KILLER!' I shouted.

We were a vortex, and the police could do nothing to stop us.

We shouted. Indeed, there was something to shout about.

Those bodies, those women and children stabbed to death. Why describe the floor?

Ropes had been twisted from sheets.

Get the killer!

It all was reason enough for us to surround the house like we did, in a growing surge. The police could do nothing to stop us.

More than anything, it was the delight the killer had taken in his work that made us shout. His hunger for crime in that room; also the way he had, still unsatisfied, arranged those poor limbs.

Get the killer!

A hurricane. We saw red.

Get the killer!

Red.

Red on my hands, which I kept hidden as I shouted.

Red as the steel in my pocket.
Get the killer!

PALERMO

I SHOULD HAVE STRANGLED my wife last night between eleven and one. Or killed them at the hour of the siesta, when no one is thinking of surprises. I should have told her I knew, because I did know.

I should have killed her last night. Strangled her, because my hands are strong. With kicks, for I know about kicks. I should have told her, then killed her. She had just put on a new necklace. She ran to the telephone without even looking at me.

I did not kill her, and I'll never be the same. I will start to lose.

I did not kill her because of today. Of this afternoon. This race.

Me, a jockey, a rider drunk on horses. Me, victorious; me, in the rapture of the wind. Calculation, heel, crop, inside the avalanche, cold and demented and coming out in front.

Me, justly famous.

What else?

It matters not.

EVEN

IN THE BAR they consult me, the calmest of men. It's true that I'm wise. Squatting at my bootblack's box, I watch the people go by. Or I polish. I know the shoes of my regular customers.

'I'm even with life,' I say, and they admire me.

I'm even, it's true.

To my son – my only child – I gave a name I'd thought about. The first one was his grandfather's name, the second, my own, the third one, the truth, for he was indeed desired. Carlos Fidel Deseado. Last name, González.

I managed to foot the bill for his studies, primary, secondary, medical school. He got his degree when he was twenty-two, and we celebrated with a roast. Not a single neighbour missed it.

That night a tram killed him.

'Twenty-two,' I said.

It's taken me thirty years to take revenge. Poison. One by one, until reaching twenty-two. Who'd suspect me? My sister's granddaughter completed the count.

I'm even with life, it's true. Calm, I watch the people pass. The waiters consult me. I am wise. I give advice with a cold heart.

ERIC GUNNARDSEN

For Gui

A YOUNG MAN was thrown out of a house surrounded by a fence. It was in Italy, by a lake. The young man left at daybreak, without a glance at the statues or a goodbye to the trees. The gate of the fence closed with a double resonance: the slide of the bolts, and the twin spears vibrating as they met.

In the city of Buenos Aires, there's a street where the wind blows and the air moves even on the calmest afternoons. One evening it flapped the coat of a woman walking up that steep street, looking for a church. When she saw it she felt relief. Its architecture calmed her, in the same way it's calming to hear one's native language spoken in an unknown region.

The church rested a step back, like a parishioner who presses her elbows to her body so as not to brush against the other devout. Two short iron railings separate the entrance from the street. This was the Dansk Kirke, the Danish church. It differed as much from neighbouring houses as the arriving woman, collar tight against her throat, differed from those leaning on the doorframes watching her pass.

The pastor, with his dry mouth and shiny forehead, was as familiar to her as the church.

She'd come to ask about a parishioner. When the pastor told her he didn't know him, she seemed entirely disconcerted. To console her, he said he'd ask his wife, though he knew his wife to be almost completely ignorant about most things.

Face pressed against the windowpane, she looked at the pavement in the evening. She saw how some women had made a mountain of trash in front of the church, and how this was lit on fire. She thought she saw an attack take place and turned to look for the pastor, but when she didn't find him, she went on looking. The wind swept away the smoke, carrying off scraps without anyone thinking of running after them. She saw the indifference of everything and asked herself what territory she'd arrived at, in search of her brother.

Upstairs, the pastor's wife was flipping through magazines from her homeland, with their pictures of brides and dated advertisements. The pastor came and held out the name of his visitor in handwriting like fly's feet. He had written it to give an impression of solicitude, also to allow the visiting lady time to compose herself. His wife asked if it wasn't the name of a physicist and astronomer, a nobleman decorated by the throne; he had been ambassador in Rome, where he had died and been buried according to his wishes in the city's non-Catholic cemetery. The pastor went silent. Then he forced her to arrange her hair and go downstairs.

When she entered the office, the pastor's wife noticed something neither her husband nor the women outside had noticed: the newcomer's beauty.

This beauty belonged to the genre of pearls, a beauty that could only be perceived with close examination, if it weren't for the grace of movement which often goes with it. Her delicacy of features might have been considered negligible had other tones composed it. But if one can use the word grey to describe the smoky hues of oyster, and plush to describe emerging antlers and lichen, one might also say there are faces modelled in grey, and that their loveliest notes are the bags under the eyes, a shadow sometimes extending to the eyelids. In such hazy facial landscapes, the eyes are often of an intense sky blue. Turquoise, almost. They also have an expression of lordly dereliction. Children like this often give forth a radiance which captivates some, and also makes their mothers wistful, fearful they will be snatched early from life. When age or some other reason softens this touch, the mothers put their fears to rest. The pastor's wife noted all this in a flash.

Behind the altar of the Danish church there are three stained-glass windows: Christ at the well with the

Samaritan woman, Saint Peter sinking in the waters and, in the largest at the centre, the multiplication of loaves and fishes. These seem to propose a charade. Seated in one of the pews, which do not allow kneeling, surrounded by a black flock of books that were familiar to unknown hands, the woman who had just arrived tried to resolve it. She did.

Passing in front of the pastor and his wife without seeing them, she went out into the wind of the night. At the corner she found her brother.

He made her enter an inn full of sailors and climb a staircase. In a room with a bed and trunk, there was a table with cheese, a knife, a bottle of spirits.

They sat in two chairs. He filled a glass halfway, cut a piece of cheese. They didn't dare look at one another.

He put the piece of cheese on a paper and pushed it towards her. She couldn't eat, just as she couldn't talk. He stopped, took her by the back of the neck, pushed the cheese between her teeth, and then the glass, forcing her to swallow. The spirits trickled down her coat. Like a drowning victim just before the waters close over her head, she looked at his cursing mouth. She wondered if its curves, which had once dazzled with their grace, could ever return. She wanted to resurrect the old outline. Like a dog that digs, trying to retrieve a prey, she started covering it with kisses.

At daybreak, she saw the window. She saw it gave onto a colonnaded pavement where scraps of papers flew about. On the table, the cheese, the bottle; the floor stained by the spirits. Then she saw her brother on the trunk. She saw his muscles, as alien to the body she had known as the line of the mouth was to its former shape. They once again hurtled themselves over one another.

On the dirty pillow, two heads like pearls argue.

I was faithful. And you married?

I was faithful. With what women did you lose yourself?

They ate on that table. Now they could look into each other's eyes.

There was a time when they'd been called the twins of sun and moon, since they'd looked almost the same. Now he stooped to eat, his nails encrusted in black; he accompanied his meal with spirits.

The two had arrived the day before, she from Copenhagen and he from the south. (He pointed vaguely with his knife.) Seven years. He insulted her; seven years without looking for him. His hands trembled on the table. She leaned forward, bathed them with her tears.

After wrapping up the leftovers of the meal, he went towards the trunk, which had a complicated lock. When the lid hit the wall she saw some rags, which he removed. The trunk was full of gold.

*

On the king's birthday, the Danish ambassador gives a reception for the whole collective. From the corner she occupied every year with her husband, the pastor's wife saw a man on the balcony dressed in black tie, just like all the others who went afterwards to the opera. When the ambassador spoke with him he abandoned his nonchalant attitude, and one could see they were friends. Afterwards, he leaned back again.

The pastor's wife crossed the salon and asked if he was Eric Gunnardsen, the son of Eric Gunnardsen. She could barely get the words out. He replied that he was. His abruptness was not benevolent but his beauty impressed her, and so she continued her effort: she wanted to know if his sister had found him. The response took a moment to come: yes, she had. Good, then she wished for them both to know she was ready to follow them wherever they liked. All they had to do was let her know at the church.

You'll have your chance, madam, at 10 a.m. on 10th March, at the railway station where the train to Entre Ríos departs, he said. He noticed the pastor approaching, and he added, raising his voice, 'Of course, you will have to bring the church harmonium with you.'

Once he had been introduced, the pastor asked the man about his sister. In Denmark with her husband, also in Italy buying statues. This said, Gunnardsen looked at his watch, bowed briefly, and went to say goodbye to his friend.

On 10th March it rained. The rain began at four, when the pastor's wife left her necklace and the money she'd saved up to visit Denmark on the table. She went out and opened the gate.

At the station she waited without moving. At ten she dared begin to walk, and made an appearance at the bar.

At a table surrounded by men were Eric Gunnardsen and his sister. A pile of big photographs sat beside the cup he was drinking from. Steam rose off raincoats, umbrellas trickled puddles on the floor.

Standing next to the table, the pastor's wife could see they were shots of the same building, park and gate. One of the men was handed photos of ironwork, another, shots of windows, the third, views of the garden. There were pictures of interiors with wall hangings piled up in front of an old man who repeated several times that he was not a magician but an antiquarian, without anyone smiling. The main conversation was carried out in Italian, with a man who appeared to be an architect.

The woman lifted her eyes and looked at the pastor's wife without recognising her. A question from her brother distracted her.

'What door is this?'

'It's new, just put in last summer.' He tore up the photos in anger, threw the pieces on the ground. 'I asked you to reproduce everything exactly,' he said to the architect. 'Balustrade by balustrade, fountain by fountain, tree by tree.'

He too lifted his eyes to the pastor's wife, failed to recognise her. She stuttered in her language. 'The king's birthday. I've brought the harmonium.' He seemed not to understand. Suddenly he leaned back and let out a guffaw.

The pastor's wife understood: it had been a joke. But she felt happy because he was laughing.

In the train, the sister went to bed. To protect the siblings from the waiter's intrusion, the pastor's wife received the dishes. Eric Gunnardsen sat at his sister's feet. So the pastor's wife wouldn't understand them, or maybe out of habit, they spoke in Italian. She did understand a bit, though.

The sister had arrived that morning. The sleeping compartments were crammed by her trunks. The pastor's wife had had to open one of them to exchange the railway company's linen for fresh sheets, to extract the pillow covered in satin as opalescent as the shoulders which rested on it.

In her student days, the pastor's wife had once seen in a museum some cutlery made of gold and mother-of-pearl. She felt a sort of kinship between that cutlery and

Eric Gunnardsen. Except for one thing, something like the feeling one gets when holding a fish-hook: a regret.

'How are they all doing there?' he asked with a mocking smile.

She described a ceremony. Beneath the pines there had been an altar, and there had been fruit garlands on the doors. Their poor first cousin had been so ugly in her red ringlets and tulle veil.

'How touching,' he said. 'Just like your wedding.'

The pastor's wife noticed the blushing against the satin pillow.

No, muttered the sister; she had been married in Copenhagen.

She rushed to continue.

A story spread about that cousin's garden wedding. People in town said they saw our parents in marvellous finery. Eric Gunnardsen sat up straight. Why was she talking about that? Did something or someone remain in that house or park that could matter to them? Who were they going to leave the tomb for? The aunt, the cousins? What an idiotic story. How dare she repeat it.

Another conversation referred to a certain dog, Tiger. She should have dug him up, he said. She should have brought him here, bone by bone, tooth by tooth. Hadn't he howled in the early morning of his departure until all the windows were opened? Hadn't he died an hour later? Anyway, he had shown more feeling than she had, oh yes, some more indeed. I only did it to save tears, she said, and they started to fall. The pastor's wife stayed outside. She saw Eric Gunnardsen kneel, turn out the light, close the door.

While construction lasted they lived in a house on the slope overlooking the river. Camps were set up for builders, gardeners, farmhands. Ships slowed their progress so passengers could watch the work. Eric Gunnardsen ordered adult trees bought, transported with giant blocks of earth at the roots. Some died and he replaced them with younger samples. At night he rose to watch over them.

At the railway station he sent back a hundred stair steps, saying he didn't want new marble. Moss-covered tiles arrived, bought from demolitions. He wrapped vines on the balconies before the work was ready, protecting them with tarps that gave everything the look of a ship.

A park surrounded the house. A railing surrounded the park.

The siblings spent hours on horseback. They went fishing; they returned from the jetty climbing the terraces between stone lions. From what the pastor's wife thought she could understand, they always spoke to one another of a certain past, a certain people.

One rainy morning she missed the pastor. She tried to sing some hymns but could not. She heard the steps of a horse on the stones. Eric Gunnardsen was looking at her through the barred window, his hair wet. Those were the months she found frightening, the months the sister was away in Denmark.

He dismounted, entered, sat at the harmonium, poked fun at the hymns. He forced her to remember old songs, songs from her wet nurse. She sang with a deep voice she hadn't used for years. He sang along softly. A smile began to form on his lips. She watched the curve appear like a rainbow in a rainy twilight, trying not to breathe so it would not disappear.

At night Eric Gunnardsen walked from room to room. The servants saw him turn on the light in the windows, and saw him on the balconies, sitting on the balustrade of the rooftop terrace with a bottle in hand. No one wanted to be the one to deliver his sister's letters. Some he tore without opening, and the wind carried away the pieces.

When she returned, things became calmer. The walks began again, the embraces beneath the trees.

On 23rd March 1926 the ambassador had the pleasure of ascending the deck of the most luxurious transatlantic liner of the period, preceded by his secretary. Sitting in the salon, he waited.

It pleased him to reply to his old friend Eric Gunnardsen, to carry out a task and accept an invitation. He was old and he loved music; he observed humanity, admired beautiful women. He observed, without pleasure but with interest, the grey-haired woman who stepped over the ground as if each splinter of wood had been created for her; he considered her husband, with his too-new clothes, for whose speeches in Parliament he felt contempt. He cast a sweeping glance at the arrangement of a red-headed daughter with a thick waist followed by a lethargic young husband and two tall brothers. Eric's uncles and cousins. The full stream of his liking went to the conservator of the collections of medals and coins of the realm and his wife, whom he knew because she was Eric Gunnardsen's sister. Three cars from the embassy awaited.

He had selected a boat from the river fleet for his friend's guest; it had seemed pleasant to him. He did not regret his choice. But the people he preferred made themselves scarce; the numismatist and his wife kept to their berth. There was no shortage of conversational topics. The grey-haired woman interrogated him about the life and personality of his brother's son. Did he still play the piano better than anyone? Did he compose? The ambassador discovered he didn't know much.

One evening he saw the one he had hoped to see more regularly at the dining table approach. When he greeted her, he commented on the appearance of the river, unusual for the time of year. She followed his gaze, seemed to remember something. She told him of the mountain of trash in front of the church, and the wind that swept away the scraps without anyone thinking of looking for them. 'What sort of lands are these?' she asked.

The ambassador thought a while, distracted by the shape of the hand by his side. Then he said, 'Maybe they are a place where souls can still fly.'

'Or lose themselves,' said a voice. It was the grey-haired woman.

A high bright light illuminated Eric Gunnardsen from behind when he welcomed his guests. The ambassador noticed a hush had fallen. The brother-in-law broke it with a laugh. Was he dreaming? – he asked – Was this house not another house, this park another park? Why not? – Eric led them to the terrace, the moon was on the river. Everything in the north can also be in the south, except in the south the water turns the opposite direction in the drains, the waxing moon seems to wane and autumn is sweeter than spring.

The member of Parliament said with a stridulous voice that those waters came from a river, not a lake. True, admitted Eric Gunnardsen, and that is an advantage: the lake keeps but the river erases. Just like the jungle. He pointed: 'As soon as we allow it to, it will cover the railings and the statues.'

The pastor's wife kept away from the visitors. During the ambassador's stays she didn't even go out of her room to eat. But that night she followed them from door to door. Her boss had behaved in an unusual manner, watching over the meals and the drinks, choosing flowers for the table. He had also delivered a packet to her wrapped in newspaper, telling her to open it the next day. She still had it in her hands. It was heavy.

The light fell fully onto the head of Eric Gunnardsen, and onto the head of the numismatist. They eyed one another. He had been looking forward to meeting him – said Eric – his sister's man, the one who spends his life examining medals. She winced, clutched her husband's arm. The husband was unfazed. He smiled; he had come from afar, he said, to find himself face to face with a double numismatic enigma: a house and a park that were the reverse of another house, another park; a man who was the reverse of a woman. Admirable obverses and reverses.

Eric Gunnardsen smiled. 'It is known,' he said, 'that heaven and hell form a single medal.' Was it to be found in the collections of His Majesty? The numismatist said that he supposed they did. But to his understanding, hell was merely an attempt to copy heaven.

The pastor's wife leaned as far as she could; she was trying to observe the grey-haired woman, who was looking at that house, that park, with a certain trembling in her features. While bending the packet fell on her foot, a sharp pain. That convinced her to open it. It was a gold ingot.

Eric Gunnardsen's speech over dessert was brief. Before he started, he invited his sister to sit by his side. She obeyed with a flutter of chiffon. He gave her wine, holding the cup up to her lips. In a lower voice he invited her to look at the centre of the table. Weren't those her favourite flowers?

He placed the watch next to the plate. Two minutes, he promised.

'A widespread belief amongst humans affirms that orphans need to receive and give affection intensely,' he said. 'When someone damages or disappoints that love, something dangerous happens. A soul is not a plaything, it is often said. Nor, unfortunately, is it a brush to white-wash tombs.'

His sister leaned against him. Seeing her close her eyes the numismatist leaped to his feet. Eric Gunnardsen stopped him. One minute, he requested. Pale, he kissed her lips and her eyelids.

'This woman will no longer know sadness,' he said. 'She is dead. Friends, cousins. One does not play with souls. I have invited you from Denmark to tell you this.'

He took out a revolver and fired a bullet into the roof of his mouth.

TWO SORRELS
AND CO.

THE CASTE OF THE SUN

IN CHIVILCOY AROUND 1942, there was a woman who was consulted often. She had golden advice for lawsuits, illness, finance and thefts, and never accepted payment. People brought her eggs or lambs, sometimes homemade jam.

She lived on the outskirts of town. One had to leave whatever means of transportation one came in parked under a pepper tree at her door.

Her hair was tied in an enormous blonde bun, which observant people noticed was a wig.

She attended to all troubles in a bureau of sorts. She would withdraw through a small double door, leaving her clients alone. A while later she returned with advice.

The rumour spread that she had a spirit in her service, and her prestige increased.

She could be seen passing in a cart drawn by a sorrel horse. To everyone's joy, someone discovered the wig was made with hairs from the sorrel's tail. The news travelled fast without reaching her ears.

When she died, they dared open the small double door. It was connected to a stable, where she kept her horse.

CRISTÓBAL THE GIANT

CRISTÓBAL WAS as big as a tree; he was a giant. He rode a huge sorrel horse. He was from the Magdalena region. His head brushed the roof beam of his *rancho* and he had to duck to go through doors. On a night of revelry, before dawn, he said to everyone, 'I wasn't born for this. I'm going to look for a chief, the greatest that exists.'

He mounted his horse and left everyone as the sun came out.

He galloped seven days and nights, looking for General Quiroga, who was in command at La Rioja. At last he found him, and said, 'Here I am, at your command, my General Quiroga.'

'Good,' said the chief. His skin was blackish, his eyes red. 'Make a big fence from boulders like tombstones so that no enemies pass. Not on horseback, not on foot, not flying.'

'I don't know much about stones, my General. I come from Magdalena. But I'll make that stone wall while my horse rests. And then the two of us will be ready for whatever you wish to order.'

The sorrel didn't like La Rioja. Not the crags, not the grasses. His hooves split open but he didn't complain.

Cristóbal didn't say anything either, but got to work. He lowered stones, pushed them forward with his chest, forced his way with his knees. He threw his lasso and used his riding crop, a crop larger than any other that has ever been seen, fit for such a horse and such a rider. He made a stone wall such as there has never been and never will be. Behind it the mountain looked small. General Quiroga seemed content.

The packs of horses he brought in from outside the wall calmly got fatter. Goats grazed nearby and the warriors slept safely at night, each dream of theirs worth a hundred normal dreams. They woke up feeling strong and laughed. They were fearless people, but there they forgot the word fear itself, which sometimes creeps in as a reminder to those who are fearless.

Near the wall, the shade was broad. When one came back from battle, sweat dried out there. Those who had been wounded felt the heat of their wounds relieved, as if they were bathing in a river, or like when, at sunset, a fresh breeze starts up and lightens tiredness. The stone wall was talked about as far away as Buenos Aires. They even say the queen of England heard it mentioned by a governor of Tucumán.

'My General,' said Cristóbal, 'now I have served you.

Let me be your soldier now. My horse has rested; there are now two of us for you to command.'

'Good,' said Quiroga. 'Tomorrow we leave for battle, and you can come. We'll see the way someone from the south behaves, someone from Magdalena and his horse. Someone from a land that doesn't know about stones.'

Cristóbal's neck swelled with courage.

'Now you'll see, General,' he said, and the sorrel shook its ears.

'I will see,' said Quiroga. His hair all in curls was the colour of pitch, and his eyes were full of the blood he shed constantly. He wore a poncho with a coloured border; on its edge there was a hidden patch no eye could spot. With a silver needle and a gold thimble, Quiroga's wife had mended it in broad daylight at his house in La Rioja, so it looked just like new. He also wore a leather hat, much scraped.

They went to battle the next day, Cristóbal along with them. He did not have a rifle, but he did have a dagger as long as a man's leg. He did not have a spear, but he had hands. And he did not have bullets, but he did have a chest like an ox's. He grabbed an enemy and flipped him over, bringing down another twenty men. He took hold of Captain Bermejo and pushed him backwards, so he went flying over a cliff with his legs in the air. The flag bearer fell along with the captain and his saddle. In the depths of the river at the foot of the crags, the wet flag seemed to cry.

Cristóbal watched General Quiroga, who is afraid of nothing. He saw him laugh in battle and bite his lips with teeth red with blood. He saw him yell, jump and kill many, and this filled his soul with happiness. 'There is no chief better than this one, not here, not in Magdalena, not anywhere. It was for his service that I, Cristóbal, was born, and I am content.'

On a stormy night, they galloped through shadow. General Quiroga led in his embroidered poncho. Nothing could be seen, not the flag, not even Cristóbal, big as the crags. They travelled through a river so as not to leave marks.

'Here,' says Quiroga, 'you may dismount and rest.'

A man came up in a hurry, on horseback.

'What is it?' General Quiroga had dismounted.

'My General, with your leave, this is the cave they call the Devil's.'

Quiroga mounted again, reins in hand. With a loud voice: 'Let's continue.'

Although tired, they mounted. Nobody said anything. They only murmured, and the thunder went on thundering.

'Who is the Devil?' asked Cristóbal.

The rain fell and ran over the field. It ran over the ponchos, over the men, over the crags and cliffs. It ran over the stones and over the tails of the horses. It fell, sounding in the river.

'Be quiet,' said the men and the flashes of lightning.

'I have seen General Quiroga go pale. That means there is someone greater than him. Someone tell me where the Devil is.'

'Be quiet,' said the thunder. They all marched in silence.

In the cool morning the birds sang. A drop hung from every branch. Quiroga was thinking.

'My General,' said Cristóbal, 'I must leave you.'

'Go,' said Quiroga. 'I have no need of borrowed men. It is only thanks to that stone wall you made that you haven't had your throat slit. Don't ever cross my path again, not you and not your horse.'

A huge tear rolled down Cristóbal's face, two down his horse's.

Back in Magdalena he saw a horde, and dust that reached up to the sky. Shrieking people drove a sorry-looking herd.

Cristóbal opened a cattle gate, galloped sideways. The sorrel, excited by the stench and steam, reared up. The chief of the troop, a man with only one eye, stopped then and there.

'Who are you? Where are you going? What are you looking for?'

'I am Cristóbal, from the Magdalena. I am looking for the Devil.'

'Come with us. And don't ask questions.'

It was dusk in a field larger than any other field, either actually seen or even dreamed of. Those sad-looking herds arrived from all directions. The horizon moved as they stumbled along, bleating. Not the ground, not the land, not even a blade of grass could be seen. Only cattle and the sound of hooves.

The riders punished their charges with relish, and hooted mockery with a sound like that of a coypu in the wetlands.

'The boss is over there. You can go and talk to him.'

Pampa stirrups, serious face. In each boot was a foot, in each foot was a claw. Wherever that claw touches, two blazes flare. Wherever that eye looks, the heart stops.

'I am the Devil. Who are you and what do you want?'

'Cristóbal, from the Magdalena. I have come to do your bidding.'

'I need a man like you, a giant. I am the owner of the world, and often need orders carried out.'

'An honour for me.'

Cristóbal took off the hat he wore, flat as a table and wide as is the style in Magdalena. His sweeping greeting fanned the fields and made a cloud of dust fly into the sea. This became an island: Martín García.

'If you serve me as you must, you'll have a prize that never ends, in my palace where torches burn.'

Here the Devil laughed, showing the black canines he uses to bite what is most secret in the heart of man.

'I do not want prizes, my lord. It is enough to serve you. There are two of us at your orders, counting my horse. This sorrel has a good trot and good character.'

Cristóbal grasped his lasso with his left hand, rolling it into four loose turns with the right, to let it fly when necessary. Thus he began his work for the Devil.

He worked no less than five years, lassoing hind-quarters and forelegs, moving about, galloping and whirl-ing his poncho round to hold the most stubborn at bay. Some he bumped down with his sorrel; they fell with a crunching of bones. He branded them with the Devil's sign. He drove them through a door by the strength of his riding crop alone.

No need to say more about that door. Inside there was very little light. Yelling and wailing came from there, and the laughter of the farmhands. Also, another louder laugh.

When the five years were over, Cristóbal presented himself to the Devil.

'Boss, if the way I serve pleases you, give me more work. My horse and I are capable of greater undertakings.'

'Make me some corrals. Five of them.'

Cristóbal unsaddled his mount. Then he began to dig, pushing, forcing open, pulling with his lasso. He spat and kneaded the mud at each edge, making corrals without walls, sunk in the earth, as there is no stone in Magdalena, and almost no trees.

The Devil went and looked. The tassel of his beret danced; he seemed well pleased.

'Not one will escape from here.'

He took out a horn whistle and blew it. The herdsmen and the one-eyed man arrived.

'The corrals are done. Let's celebrate with a roast.'

Off they went, and there was a smell of charred hide, so black the day turns into night. Amongst them, Cristóbal and his horse.

On the road that goes from Pila to Ranchos there lived a widow, the mother of ten children. A single tree gave shade to her *rancho*. She had hens, but they'd left to lay their hatch by a wire fence. The youngest of her daughters didn't reach higher than a horse's leg, but she knew how to mount with knees and hands. Each morning she'd ride saddleless. She dismounted at each nest and put the eggs in her plaid handkerchief. Then, she mounted again. Not a single egg was ever broken inside that plaid handkerchief.

From Pila to Ranchos went galloping the Devil with his people. They were thinking of the roast.

Nearby, a hen got upset with the widow's daughter and pecked her finger, making her jump. The tin cross she wore revealed itself in a silvery flash.

The Devil halted, with a sharp yank on the reins. Foam spurted from his lips.

'I can't go through!'

He kicked against the horse, and the horse kicked against the ground.

'We can't go through!'

The demons, drooling, formed a swamp. They boiled, bubbling, like a cooking pot of pitch at its most fervent point.

'What is it?' asked Cristóbal.

'Something that is something,' said the one-eyed man, his tongue lolling out.

'Something that is what?'

'It cannot be named.'

The girl's cross flashed again. With an awful cry the Devil went racing away, and behind him the the rest of the screaming lot.

Only Cristóbal and his sorrel remained.

Slowly, so as not to scare her, he approached the girl wrapping eggs in the plaid handkerchief.

'Who is that lord you carry on your neck?' he asked, removing his hat.

'Ask Father Pedro, at the ruins.'

She pointed with her finger. Nothing but a long horizon could be seen.

There Cristóbal made his way on his horse, after both took a drink from the watering hole.

Father Pedro sat alone at that ruin the Indians had destroyed twice. So many dead friars! Crying out to God, their souls and their rosaries had been wrested from them.

Cristóbal dismounted, and made his greeting, tipping his hat low. The friar was very small and very pale.

'What brings you here?' came his question.

Cristóbal told him, because he was always well disposed. He told him how he had gone looking for a chief, how he had served Quiroga, how after that he had served the Devil. And what had happened when the girl leaped and the tin cross shone.

The friar smiled and invited him to share a maté. They talked of worldly things, and of what is sacred.

'How may I serve that Lord then?' asked Cristóbal, holding out his two hands.

Father Pedro said to him, 'Fill the corrals you made for the Devil with water. Where there is water, there is no thirst. There is joy. Birds come, and people and cattle can rest.'

Cristóbal galloped away. He filled the hat with water from the Salado River. He poured it into a corral until it spilled over.

'How foolish you are!' cried a lapwing. 'Good water is fresh! Who is going to drink that salty stuff?'

That lagoon remained salty, but Cristóbal filled the other four with fresh water. Now they have names.

After his work was done Cristóbal reached the sky with one gallop. The Lord thought him very generous, and his sorrel very handsome. They can be seen drawn in the stars, looking content. Friends of men, of beasts, of good water and of willingness.

TASKS

CANGALLO STREET

O F MY CHILDREN I prefer the middle ones. They were born while I was in Ushuaia. A cold place without news, because I don't know how to write and neither does my wife. She is a laundress.

When I served my time, I came back. She got up as if to quarrel. My two first children were there. There were also two more playing on the floor.

I sat down, and she served me a meal. Afterwards, we looked at each other. Then I looked at the children, one by one, the first two, and those two others. I liked them.

I cried, she cried too. A few years had passed, and it showed. In time, we had others. Now there are six of them. That is something, six. Six children.

Inclined as I am to get angry, to drink, I refrained from another crime. Not because of the thought of Ushuaia, but because of those middle ones. Not because they were good-looking, unlike poor me, an ugly mulatto. Not because they were a blond boy and girl, and happy, not, like me, sad. Not because of anything. I just prefer them, and they love me.

I sell newspapers for the six of them, coughing in this street I hate, every night until dawn. But if anyone passing sees me smile, it's because I'm thinking of the middle ones.

AN EMBROIDERER

DIEGO PÉREZ, an embroiderer by trade, died burned by the Inquisition in Lima. Fleeing from it, he left Madrid. In the street of the embroiderers, only one noticed his departure and went to see him off, crying.

The way he embroidered can be imagined from the silks of the games room at the royal pavilion in Aranjuez. A pale testimony, for throughout all the centuries nothing from that prodigious street can be compared to the embroideries he made.

He only found peace while embroidering. When he arrived in Buenos Aires, he did not dare offer his services to the viceroy or bishop, and instead worked for a harness maker. But his hands were not made for that. They flew over silk or velvet. He dedicated his free hours to embroidering a mantle of the Virgin of Carmen the English took away in 1806.

Did he have bad luck?

He was naive. It's difficult to picture him as a heretic. His agony began with a confidence. He told a colleague that as a young man, he had embroidered cloth. But that now there was no difference between the embroiderer and the embroidered, that when embroidering he was embroidered, that the embroidery embroidered him and he the embroidery. The colleague – the one who had cried when seeing him off – thought about that. At last he denounced him for witchcraft. It weighed heavy on him, as he admired him.

In Lima he met with the accusation once again. He shouted, 'I'm innocent!' over and over again. They burned him.

As they swept away his ashes, he appeared before the Inquisitor, and before his colleague in the street of embroiderers. They saw him, luminous, waving like a banner, hands deformed by the needle, black from the fire, throwing out rays of light through the spikes of Christ. The game hunts and meadows he had embroidered ran through him.

He vanished, with a smile.

CHACARITA

I TALKED WITH BUONARROTI from the first moment. With these eyes that marble dust makes red, I touched his works one by one, in the places his hands had touched.

To emigrate does not mean to forget. On 13th November 1901 I arrived in Buenos Aires.

While I work, I ask him, 'Is this how you think? Well, I think this way.'

I am an artist and creeds don't concern me. I made grieving figures on truncated columns, the sepulchres of freemasons. Angels and Ladies of Sorrow with a cross alongside. The wreaths I brought forth from the stone seemed to breathe. A whole village sprang from my two hands.

Every breath I take is for art. It's the substance on which I nourish myself. I know the acidity of jasper and how to awaken alabaster.

Yesterday two young people, art students by the looks of it, nudged each other in the ribs while passing my door.

'From this place,' said one, 'issues part of what makes this cemetery so comic.'

The other laughed, an extraordinary laugh.

I won't talk with Buonarroti any more. Now I will work in silence.

LADY MUSIC

THERE'S NO REASON to think the cap and whistle had always been everything in Enrique Bomon's life. He was stationmaster, calm, with pale eyes. He never attended union meetings. The union proposed him as a delegate. He did not accept.

His life was a poor one. He was saving, some said. I don't believe it.

He sat on the ground without smoking and made a little sound, the representation of a music that for him was complete.

Now you'll see why. The world is full of twists and turns.

A couple of foreigners approached him on the plat-form. His beard was grey, but his posture was good and he looked serene. Leaning forward, he listened, neither confirming nor denying. He smiled.

The woman, above all, was agitated. She'd blushed when she got off the train, her husband behind her. Enrique Bomon showed no sign that he had either recog-nised or forgotten her.

Some women are like that. She had herself taken to

the editorial department of a newspaper. She unleashed the reporters.

Around that time he changed his job, and began to work as a gatekeeper. Perhaps it was to avoid them.

If we begin to look closely, his chronology in reverse is as follows. All this is true: he played bass drum in the city band of Junín in '98. Before that he was seen as a farmer in Zárate and wall painter in Pergamino. He'd opened a music shop when he arrived in Buenos Aires in 1874. Where had he come from? Australia and South Africa, where he was a miner, a seeker of diamonds.

Why a music shop? There's the key. Let's look at his chronology the other way around.

Birth: Brussels, 1849. At eight years old, the Royal Conservatory awarded him a position as soloist. He was called a prodigy. In what? The cello. Servais, his teacher, cried when listening to him later, when Paris, Berlin and London gave him their blessings. One night, in Rio de Janeiro, Emperor Pedro II summoned him to his box seat. Without speaking he held his gold watch towards him.

Another night approached. He'd just emerged from a concert, and was looking at the stars above the palaces. The music in him had condensed into full expression. There would be no more instruments. No more public. No more expressing, seeking or serving her. She was within him.

Lady Music.

Another life went on.

All that remains is to explain the nomadism, the adventures. Who knows? Perhaps he felt a thirst for other identities, once his steely apprenticeship had ended. Perhaps he hoped to dissolve in non-identity.

The fact is: these chronologies are real.

Something else remains: his name. Enrique Bomon. Henri Beaumont, de Beaumont? The transcription of a customs employee erased his origin. And this delighted him.

J.M. KABIYÚ FECIT IN YTAPUÁ, 1618

INDIAN BRUTE, I heard myself called for this. It's true I am one, but not for this.

I painted him on his knees. The drops on my forehead pricked like the thorns I painted on His.

I painted someone else, kneeling as well. Tears ran down my face thinking of him.

Indian brute, I heard myself called for this. It's true I am one, but not for this.

Not for painting Judas, crying, on his knees.

WHITE FLOWERS

WHITE FLOWERS RAINED on Buenos Aires the night Juan Arias was born. Few saw them, even fewer caught their scent. Who knew if they were there because he was being born? Not even his mother, who didn't even see them. Besides, she died right after he came into the world.

Someone in a lonely apartment saw them descending through the night and asked, 'Who's being born?' or 'Who's dying?' That was it.

We've already said it. Juan Arias was born. There's not much to add about his life. If he'd been rich, he would have played the role of a gentleman. But he was poor. And though he was very beautiful, he was considered an idiot.

In old age he was given the work judged most appropriate to him: locating cars in a Diagonal Norte parking garage. He did this with care, just like everything else.

There he died one night. Softly, in spite of the rain.

TACHIBANA

No one brought more money to the house on Suipacha Street than little Flora, or Tachibana. It was 1892. Her science of the senses was astonishing.

Gentlemen – politics and alcohol – discussed her at the club. One proposed marriage. As if they were no more than a handkerchief, he offered her his lands, big enough to hold a hundred Japans in them. Another one, tall and blond, fought a duel for her, killing his father-in-law and then himself.

Little Flora, or Tachibana, occupied herself with the Chan'g, the great doctrine without doctrine. In the mornings she meditated: 'Who were you before your parents were born?' The thought suffused her until she felt the boundaries between herself and her room dissolve.

Well, as is known, on a certain date, at ten in the evening, she attended to the Vice President of the Republic. They toasted. The soft clink of glasses seemed to burst in her ear like the sound of a hundred volcanos. She saw herself reverberating like the leaves and the houses and the monsters and the planets and the murmurs in the fountain.

They say that she came down the staircase, her face shining. She laughed in front of the madam, stretching out both her arms.

It's not that she didn't go back to work. She did, but now she was invulnerable.

TRAINS

For Manuel Mujica Láinez

THE GREAT NIGHT
OF THE TRAINS

A ROUND THE TIME man first set foot on the moon, it rained hard in Buenos Aires. The trains put out to die dripped and water ran unceasingly down the windowpanes.

The government had decided to amputate the railway lines, just as doctors dry out unhealthy veins from the calf. It put the old trains on one side of the tracks to die.

Most of the wagons' windows were broken, and puddles formed on the seats and on the floors. The thistles formed a forest, their little heads hitting the glass like a crowd cheering a king. The earth gave way and the trains felt they were sinking. If they didn't feel water seeping into their core it was because they were made of the hardest wood in the world, from India.

The rebellion of the trains took place that month.

There were two causes: the lack of sun, and the purchase of yellow trains by the government.

The insufficiency of sunlight in those months, to talk like an academic, undermined the moral energies of the trains put out to die. During that time they were unable to wake from their dreams. In addition, there was none of the heat that usually radiated through the planks, the same way a smile radiates. There was no blue.

When there is blue, tatters can wave without feeling wretched; they can feel they are banners or anything else. Maybe the term 'tatter' will surprise someone who remembers the old train roofs' blackness, a superb blackness. But the roofs were made of cloth, as was evident when, after a period of abandonment, they began to turn grey and tear.

It must be understood that trains dream, just like the whole world apart from hens.

The dreams of the trains put out to die were long as a result of their leisure, and wide-ranging as a result of their age. The first-class wagons with leather seats didn't have the same dreams as the wagons in second with wooden seats. But their memories were of equal importance to them.

One had been a restaurant with tablecloths, dinner service and waiters. Another had been a sleeping car.

Those were their memories. Their dreams were more varied, more confusing and more difficult to explain.

These dreams worked as leavening for the rebellion.

Without sun, the trains didn't wake up. Nor did they have the usual activity around them that makes life acceptable, not even plants. The buzz of bees can be important in certain circumstances.

What they did have were months of water, thunder, water, more water, more thunder, more water. The roads became tongues of mud no one would travel, not men, not trucks, not cattle, not anything. Everything was loneliness, leaking, dripping, silence. The trains put out to die felt something awful was going to happen.

Twice a week the diesels returned them to the world. There had never been conflicts with the diesels, or if there had been, there's no need to call attention to conflicts that are natural in any new start. For years they had shared the service equally. The flaming hues of the diesel-powered trains had gradually toned down to the earthy dispositions more appropriate to real trains; that alone was enough to make them trustworthy. Also, even without an engine worthy of the name, they carried out their duty with spirit.

During the watery months, it was they who reminded the trains put out to die of their condition as denizens of this world. Twice a week they shook off the density of their dreams. They were the ones that revealed that the government had purchased the yellow trains.

This was the second cause of the rebellion. But one must not think the yellow trains had the slightest contact with or were even aware of the existence of the trains put out to die. They only serviced the lines travelling immediately north, the ones we use when we go to place a bet in San Isidro, sunbathe in Olivos or ride the ferry in Tigre. This note does not imply they are frivolous. Thousands of people live in the zones they pass through, and I believe even newspapers have taken it upon themselves to photograph the excessive work they must do, the bunches of people hanging off their sides or piling up on their roofs during their daily route.

None of which can even be imagined on the lines of the south, where the rebellion happened. There, it's common for a train to stop because a cow is asleep on the rails. On those journeys, setting your bag down on the nettings sometimes sends up a cloud of thistle flowers, which land softly on the clothes of the nearest passenger.

No one knows how the rebellion was organised. It's unclear whether or not the diesel engines played an active role. Since they continued to be used, one might believe they had no pressing motives. But alerted to a terrible fate by their friends put on the railway sidings, it is probable that they participated surreptitiously.

It seems the rail carts were more involved than one later knew. Maybe because of their contact with the rail-repair crews, men much given to bragging, the carts often made cutting remarks at the trains put out to die. As the carts lack windows, doors and, to put it plainly, every-thing else, it didn't upset them to see the shades pulled off the trains, those that could once be lowered over the windows to sift the light. Dust would dance through the air of the wagons in ceremonial displays, stairways of light and shadow created by the blinds, so gorgeous that a journey of seven hours could pass in a single breath for an attentive traveller. It did not pain the carts either to see the panes broken on some of the doors, smoked glass that had featured sketches and railway initials, made at a time decoration was considered one of the obligatory pleasures of life. Rapid and impudent, with nothing to lose, they made an effort to encourage the spread of the mutiny, helping place certain locomotives, delivering news.

In those days a few wagons were set on fire near Constitución. The aim was to take advantage of their iron and steel. You've seen them: a criminal impression. It couldn't have happened at the stations farther away, where the country folk are poor because the trains pass so rarely, and no one thinks of making off with a seat or mirror for their *ranchos*.

Little is certain, but it's known that the trains' meeting place was a station on the abandoned line to Magdalena.

It was a good place because of its isolation and because it was a symbol.

It is still there; anyone who likes can go and see it today. Thistles, wind, a shed at each lonely station. The wooden brackets through which once cows, rearing their heads and pushing one another, boarded the trains, stand empty. Only the swallows, if they feel like it and it's summer, or perhaps the bats, happy at sundown, go through them. If I could fly, I'd go take a look too. Not otherwise. At the ticket booth, a written sign sways in the wind. A door opens, closes, makes the heart beat faster, but there's nothing to worry about; it's just a door the wind bangs shut. There are devices in the offices, stuck at settings of their own choosing. Truth is they are not really interested in any setting at all. As for the tale about a puma that dwells at the stationmaster's, it's false. There haven't been any pumas in the region for almost a century. I'm ready to believe, yes, the one about the dead ewe, stinking on the oaken staircase. Also, that an occasional calf can suddenly burst out of the waiting room. Now, if you wish to think it's a wild cat rather than a puma, you will probably be right. You could possibly find a tramp too, although they are not as abundant there as in other parts, westward.

What I wouldn't give to have seen that night, the great night of the trains.

La Indómita hurtled from the broken sheds of Ranelagh station, belching smoke. It was raining that night, and smoke pressed itself against the sides and wheels of the train. The lights looked yellow in the nocturnal steam.

There was La Olga, licence number 7.897, her radiance different from that of all the rest. Crowned by her ray of light, she appeared, a knower of snows, one who, sheathed in whiteness, had arrived at the platforms of Bariloche and Neuquén. She used to tell stories which were as true as they were hard to believe.

La Rosa arrived in the beam of a headlight. There was a moment of respectful observance. More than all the others, it is she I would like to have seen, tearing through the gates of Circunvalación station and advancing surrounded in sparks that the rain put out and put out again. Her licence plate, sadly erased, dragged long strands of vines. In 1918, when she was still new and terrible, she challenged the army and police. Driven by rioting anarchists, flags screaming in the wind, she swept down the line like a black bonfire.

La Morocha came and waited for orders. She knew a thing or two, after having pulled the wagon with couches used by the President of the Republic, and also the trains used during the sugar harvest, full of Indians from Bolivia who played the flute on human bones. Once she transported the second elephant that had ever come to the country, which never lost its dignified manner despite its distrust of rail travel. It was thanks to La Morocha's serenity that there were so few deaths in the derailment of February '46. Now she made her way in silence; her whistle was too well known.

And among them the main one moved, silent.

How much work it must have been, and how difficult, how much coming and going.

To call together those locomotives, some active but blind, others enthusiastic but stripped of a vital part. The rail carts came and went, the diesel engines ambled along. And the trains put out to die in the rain in the ferment of their dreams, wanted to wake from everything, straining with a groan which shook them to their very core.

And wake they did.

The rails were slippery that night, as well they might have been. Imagine the skidding, the difficulties braking, the challenges getting started. Also, everyone was fed up with the rain, which was an advantage. Hardly anyone poked a head out of their house, and after every thunderbolt a little old lady lying in bed said, 'Lord, protect the walkers.'

As to whether there were crashes, yes there were, and this was anticipated. No one could control the signals. The express from Bahía Blanca was destroyed, and La Rosa along with it, a wheel turning blindly on the side where the Anarchist flag had waved in '18.

On the Samborombón Bridge, where fishermen have planted poplars for shade, for some unknown reason one of the biggest trains, full of sleeping cars, derailed. Usually there is little water there; its riverbed seems intended for ten rivers just like it. Despite the rains it was only half empty. But there was enough water to rush into the splintered berths at the bottom of the gorge.

Ah, but let's imagine the trains put out to die.

To feel once again the hitch, the sound of irons, the violent shake that joins one wagon, then another, then another. A groaning noise. Some planks split, something else is smashed in.

Some couldn't get away. They crashed or slipped in the night, without the light of fireflies because of the rain.

But many could.

It is because of those I would have liked to be there. To see them back on the rails, breathing once more, the engine at the lead, the telegraph posts whisking past. Being trains again.

Yes, it is because of them I wish I'd been there.

The rebellion of the trains was great. Why it failed and who informed on it will never be clear. It doesn't matter. What matters is the flame that rises and is dampened and rises once again.

Great was that night, very great indeed.

Why it wasn't reported in the newspapers, I have already told you. Man had just walked on the moon, and the newspapers had no space for anything else.

LOVE

THE DAUGHTER of the stationmaster had a white attaché case, and when you opened the lid you could see it had a mirror. She would smile in front of it, dimples in her cheeks.

She'd polish the case with a rag dipped in milk. She'd wash the rag and hang it in the sun. She'd clean the mirror with silk paper. She wrote to her friends from school. She kept her letter paper in the case.

She had arrived from school by train, sitting between her parents. During the journey the blond railwayman had looked at her. She kept her face hidden behind the cover of the attaché case, where she saw her disturbed features reflected. 'He's not good enough for me,' she thought. He was arrogant to boot.

He sported the sort of cap favoured by city dwellers. He liked women and women went crazy for him.

She began to get up at six to try and see him, and to spy on Rosa.

Let me tell you about Rosa. She brought milk to the train in a cart high as a house. She was tall and serious as a man, was expecting a child and was madly in love with the blond railwayman, who had left her.

Hidden behind the blinds, the daughter of the station-master saw the sun come out from behind the train. She heard the chat of the milkmen who received empty jars and loaded full ones, Rosa amongst them. Sometimes she saw the rail cart pass and saw the urban cap, heading towards the station.

She kept a diary: when the young man did the rounds, when he passed in the truck with the others, how she managed to look at him without him seeing her.

She stored the diary in the attaché case, which she locked with a key that seemed golden.

One day she wrote: Rosa brought a newborn and left it on the cargo balance while she was busy with the jars. Hairless and red. Disgraceful. It's disgusting, and I hate it.

In the desert there are no secrets. The rounds of the young man at the station must have been noticed, because Rosa started to look at the window of the stationmaster's daughter, and from behind the blinds the stationmaster's daughter looked at her.

Then the big rain came. As one knows, there was no sadder time.

When it started, no one worried. But when they had to abandon their houses… The green expanse turned blue.

The stationmaster had to move his family to the city, but in front of the train his daughter refused. Like two little birds fluttering behind bars, her parents repeated: why? Because she would travel the next day. Used to obeying her wishes, they agreed.

She had a reason. The young man had stopped doing the rounds of the station, and if she remained alone she thought he would appear. All she could think of was him.

But there was no train the next day.

The radio said the rivers had burst their banks. The stationmaster's daughter remained alone at the station.

She ate a little powdered milk from a can. There were hens in the henhouse, but she didn't know how to kill them. She cried, she trembled. The telegraph tapped in the parlour. She had always refused to learn to decipher it, but now her hands struggled. Opening the suitcase, she sobbed before the mirror. How pretty her dimples were. She called the young man's name. If only he'd come to save her. But all she could hear was rain and croaking.

Afterwards the dogs appeared. Dogs from the abandoned houses, in packs, starving. They howled and jumped against the henhouse, and the hens went mad, losing their feathers. The dogs made an opening and fought over them with their teeth.

The stationmaster's daughter, hiding crouched on the floor, tore out her hair. A puddle of tears formed beside the window.

The dogs left through the gap, just as they'd entered, feathers and threads of egg yolk on their lower jaws.

Night fell, with more rain and croaking. Even the radio had gone silent.

She heard the sound of the cart on the rails, and an energetic voice that repeated her name. She jumped to the window, calling out the name of the blond young man.

Rosa was in the cart, her hooded milkmaid's cloak dripping water. She shouted, asking her to bring the lamps from the telegraph room.

The stationmaster's daughter grabbed her white oil-cloth attaché case, and hurried towards her.

Shaking her by the curls until her teeth chattered, Rosa said: the lamps. She dressed her in another hooded cloak. The stationmaster's daughter moaned and didn't let go of the case. She ran to look for the lamps in the darkness, and, intent on holding on to her case, dropped two. They shattered.

You have to keep them dry this way, said Rosa. She raised her cloak.

Sheltered beneath it, the red child slept.

The thistles had grown like trees. They grew at every moment, they crossed the rails, hindered the cart. Rosa covered the infant and jumped to clear the railway, her whip and milkmaid's lantern in hand.

The daughter of the stationmaster covered her eyes. She wept: she pulled my hair.

In the night there was rain, lightning, thistles. They passed an empty station, the wind moved the casuarina trees. Three stations left, said Rosa. Then we'll find people.

But they found dogs.

One pricked up its ears, they all pricked them up. They woke. They howled.

Tongues lolling in the wind, they ran behind the cart, they caught up with it.

Rosa lit a lamp beneath the cloak, threw it. It exploded and scorched a few noses. That bought them some time.

But soon the dogs reached them again. Panting could be heard. Nothing could be seen. Another lamp. In a confusion of yelps, the dogs withdrew. Ran faster.

The last lamp didn't light; it was wet. Dog spittle sprinkled the cart now. Rosa lashed out with her whip. Grey hairs flew. She lashed again, but a set of jaws snatched the whip, which crunched like a wood chip.

Quick, quick. When lightning struck, the pelts could be seen; a tooth clinked against the iron edge; a howl of anxious hunger could be heard.

A milkmaid's cloak flew at them through the air, heavy, reeking of cows. It was snapped up before landing and chewed up.

But the rails took a curve. Cutting across the field, the dogs arrived. Relentlessly they pursued on one side. The lantern cracks a black forehead, is smashed. The second cloak flies through the air. The cart almost flies too. Rosa takes off her skirt and covers her baby. Her underskirt is like a flag.

Oh, to fly.

A light in the station. There are people there, we are arriving. But the thistles have grown, they grow at every moment, they cross the rails, bring the cart to a halt. 'Your case, throw it!'

With bare hands she pulls out thistles.

'Let's go!'

The dogs pause to fight over the white parcel thrown to them.

Run, run.

That light is the station. We're almost there.

The dogs arrive first. One leaps. Fangs tear a shoe.

Now two shots are fired. Howling, they back away, tear away into the night. Two fall.

A locomotive splashes through the rain before coming to a stop. The blond young man jumps out, shotgun in hand. The stationmaster jumps out, the police jump out.

'Love!' shouts the stationmaster's daughter. She grabs her attaché case. She falls into the young railwayman's arms.

Love. They lock lips.
Rosa stoops. She is looking for her son.
He isn't there.

THE TRAINS OF THE DEAD

THE FAST TRAIN to Bahía Blanca dragged down the son of the foreman in charge of the rail maintenance crew. He'd been a sad man since his wife's death, and with this he gave himself over to drink.

The son spent a month as if asleep. When he returned home he wasn't the same.

He was lame, but above all distracted.

He devoted himself to lighting small bonfires, adding fuel to them day and night.

At times he raised his arms and gave a shout.

One afternoon his father came back from the bar and began to cry. What was he doing with those fires, for heaven's sake? They made the neighbours pity him.

'At the hour of the accident,' said the boy, 'I saw the trains of the dead.'

They crossed like rays of lightning above the world. Some came and others went, rising and falling without direction or destination. In the windows he saw the faces of the dead in this world. Ashen faces bearing smiles, leaning faces. Faces held in place by suffocating bits of cloth, limp hands, coloured hair. Electricians, housewives, priests, presidents of companies. Dead in life. Cheekbones covered in bone-dust. Tossing to and fro.

He saw people he knew, neighbours.

In trains shining bright as ghosts risen from the swamp. Nodding their heads, curls pressed against the glass, they did not ask for help, did not want it. Under the permanent cover of night, trains without voice or whistle passed one another, without signals, without a pattern.

They crashed or followed one another for no reason, switching lines.

Nobody could hear or see them flying above the world.

His own pain was joy compared to the pain of those in the trains. He saw, and it was as if he touched, how the cold froze those travellers in place, just as it did those who go to sleep forever in the Andes. Within the ice floes, their eyes called without calling.

That's why he had put out signals. For the trains of the dead.

EXILES

CRISTOFEROS

I DIDN'T KNOW what a sad continent I was inaugurating. The way things are now, I deserved my end.

Have you ever paused to think about the rats, about me, shackled in the darkness?

The ocean I crossed three times as an admiral, I crossed back in stench and fever, as a prisoner.

Maybe today I know what my crime was. What a continent I inaugurated!

My dust, guarded by mounted giants, is honoured as that of a monarch in a peerless cathedral, Sevilla. Today tourists take a turn around it with a squeak of shoes, guide in hand, and when they discover my name they speak it aloud.

My name! Bearer of Christ!

The truth is that chance does not exist.

At the moment of my death (it will come to you too) the last words He spoke came to my mouth.

Did a final lock click into place?

Do you ever think of what I once was, one like yourselves, fond of certain things, inflamed by the thought of others, a mad scanner of the horizon?

We know the stories of those who, like me, sought something beyond themselves in those lands. Bolívar was turned in at night by his friends, wrists in shackles. Another died an old man, before a strange sea. (Yet another, in a land without oxygen, at death's door in a room made of mud, was shot by someone sweating in terror.)

Consider – there is no such thing as chance – the effigy that a southern city raised in my honour.

With my back to the continent I mention, I look towards the sea. Behind me, invisible to my eyes, is the Star. A marble enclosure has been consecrated to a flame. According to the clauses, it should burn in perpetuity. But there is no flame. In this darkness, the employee who looks after the park where my statue stands has fashioned himself a den. His drunken shouts scare away the children who dare to peer in from the marble steps.

REFLECTION
ON THE WATER

ELVIRA CABRINI. White hair. Eighty years old. The world for her was like a landscape reflected on gold water. Each thing trembled in the glory of its reflection.

It's true that when she lost her only son she was consumed by despair. But the splendour of the world sustained her. And when she received the kisses of her last lover she could say, 'Lady Sadness, I never knew you. I only knew your nobler brother, Pain.'

Every word is heard by someone.

One day she woke, and the reflection was no longer there. Only things remained. From that day on, she'd have to experience this new state.

The words of the flowers came to her. She understood them, since she recognised them from another time. They were like the words of past love. But now they remained silent, saying nothing to her.

She remembered one evening sitting in front of a lake. Through the scattered clouds, through the herons that had begun to grow sleepy, through the flights of wild ducks, a smear, a small flutter advanced over the water. She couldn't stop looking. It was like a will-o'-the-wisp, but black, and grew larger as it came nearer. It was a boat, and in the boat stood a figure in a flowing dress. The dogs hadn't barked. The dress ballooned in the wind. Elvira, who was like a queen, stood up. The lady arrived; she wore a big hat.

Sitting beside the visitor in one of the wicker arm-chairs on the veranda, Elvira watched intently trying to see her face, to no avail.

When the lady rose to leave, Elvira was unable to get up. Not one dog stirred. The lady moved away again in her boat over the lake, towards the landscape of clouds; the cry of a coypu came from the reeds.

Afterwards Elvira went into her house. She didn't see the baby chicks that had come off the visitor's clothing. They entered through the grille of the windows, spread out through the rooms, hopped over the dogs, pecked away at hearts. They were black, diamond-beaked.

That had happened a number of years ago.

Now on her knees, her request was this: 'Just once, before dying, grant me joy again.'

It was early evening. She blew out the lamp, wanting to sleep, but the fervour of her request continued to operate like a machine that keeps on humming. Late at night she lit the lamp again, and sat beside the window.

At dawn she heard the motor of an automobile. The dogs barked.

Elvira Cabrini saw a young man with a helmet in his hand on the patio, alongside a race car splattered with mud.

It was the third time that young man could have been champion of the world, and wasn't. That afternoon was the third time. They say the heart is like a glass, and that when bitterness fills it to the brim, it overflows in tears. The young man left the city behind, racing over dirt paths and mud puddles. Headlights illuminated cow eyes, a hare, an owl. He braked far from everything, in the middle of night.

At that hour he saw a light turned on far away, Elvira's light. He went towards it, and dawn arrived.

Elvira Cabrini saw him come in. She saw the most beautiful of gods eating bread and butter before her eyes. A man told her who he was, a boy told her of his pain. Blond hair stuck to his temples, his helmet rested on a chair.

Love burned within her once again.

While he was bathing she went for a walk. She looked at the low clouds like the bellies of marvellous birds brooding over the egg-shaped lake.

The world revealed itself to her once more.

He went to sleep a siesta in the guest room, and she crowned herself with flowers before the bedroom mirror. She looked blonde, just as she had when she was young.

She died, rosy, smiling, during that siesta.

STEAM IN THE MIRROR

'TOKIO' IS THE NAME of my neighbourhood dry cleaner's. Sitting at a desk, its owner oversees the work. She hardly speaks Spanish. Amidst the steam her children listen to tangos on the radio.

The day they made me rector of the university I went to have my trousers ironed. The boys gave me a dressing gown while I waited.

Out of modesty, the mother left her post. She didn't know I teach oriental languages. I could read, on the table, what she'd been writing:

> *Here you are*
> *Mirror*
> *Four years hidden under papers*
> *A trace of beauty lingered on your waters.*
> *Why didn't you save it?*

It's worth something, I understood that afternoon, to be rector of the university, expert in oriental languages, owner of a single pair of trousers.

IN THE PUNA

W HEN YOU'RE TRANSFERRED to the Puna, think of me. I was transferred there to be headmaster of a school.

The Puna is a desert. People in the city like to listen to songs naming it. They don't know oxygen isn't breathed there, that water boils cold. Children often die on their way to school.

As far as the school goes, I've never compromised. As a teacher, my lessons were never based on rote learning. As director, I prohibited it. 'I want students, not parrots,' was my motto. Some teachers hated me; I treated them as idiots.

In the Puna life moves a different way. To be more precise: it doesn't move.

Sometimes, reading beneath the lamp, I murmur, '*Tanto gentile e tanto onesta pare…*' And beauty accompanies me.

When I get down from my mule, songs about dead lovers and the knight who cannot be named haunt me.

In bed, where I hardly sleep, I hear the three virtues named. I meditate on them: why are there three? Why these three? What are they?

Something, faint as a stroke of chalk on the black-board, is inscribed within me. Partially erased, but not entirely.

When you're transferred to the Puna (no one can escape it), the voice of memory will nourish you.

You'll regret ever having a headmaster like me, inimical to putting wheat in earth, bread of the exiled man.

JULIANO STAMPA

I WAS JULIANO STAMPA'S FRIEND until I was twenty years old. I was in love with his mother, she was in love with him.

The place where we studied had three balconies. We quickly learned how to look outside without leaning on our hands. There were roses on the sill.

An entire language flowed in from the park to that room. Like sailors in a sea of green we cast our view outward, then reeled it back in so we could study.

I felt fear, respect and admiration for Juliano. He was fierce and elegant, and never lied. His rages seemed to be a kind of lashing out. The intensity of his bad moods was unsettling.

I spent my time waiting for the moment his mother appeared. When she showed up, she would rush past to avoid us, out of sensitivity more than anything. She was just like a Hollywood actress with her sunny smile. Compassionate, musical, wary of animals. Extremely beautiful.

But that shyness, that fear of troubling anyone with her demeanour, exasperated him.

One afternoon, the rumbling of a car leaving for the station could be heard. Juliano's angst increased. His father was arriving by that train. Later I ran into him under the majestic trees of the garden. An energetic man.

Every day at dawn he conferred with my father under those trees. They stretched out their arms, pointing here and there. My father wore a straw hat. He was the gardener.

The chimneys of the Stampa factories seemed to afflict Juliano with their blackness. He made drawings of hanged or martyred men. But he never talked badly of anyone. It was himself he disliked.

I always kept to myself the little I learned about him. We would go together to the city and separate at the station, Retiro or Palermo. I went to the law faculty and he studied administration, supposedly.

Most of the time he would go to the zoo. He spent hours before the cages, drawing animals during the hour for lessons. His tigers seemed to breathe.

Other times he went to his father's factories, toured the plants, was presented to foremen. One night we drank too much, and he burst into tears.

When he was twenty he escaped. He wrote one letter from Montevideo, and another from Europe, asking to be forgiven. He gave no explanations.

In London I was able to see him.

He was a great clown.

His mother travelled regularly to see him. She couldn't help clapping, though she was afraid he'd discover her in the last row. She was a widow, and now had a younger husband. It wasn't me.

A.R.J.

THIS WAS THE LOT in store for me. Being feared did not free me, as I sometimes thought it might. Preparing myself did not make me prepared.

Someone by my side, spoon in hand, feigns patience. And I was not a poet. No, I was not. No.

Prologues, conferences. What passion amidst papers. Truth is, I was moved when, one day, I saw my name in a newspaper.

Ridiculous, I am afraid, so fat, in love with beautiful young men.

I, who have been immortal in someone's lap, had to put up with sarcasm and taxes.

Later, domestic love with someone uglier than me. (But, hadn't I dreamt of Apollo?) Spoon in hand, eyes looking longingly out the window, domestic love prepared to fly. Hadn't we cooked and got fat together? Hadn't we sworn to ourselves that we'd lose weight? We'd joke at the scales.

The smell of books, a two-room apartment on Alsina Street. A neon sign blinded the view from the window. Was this life then? What about Greece and the blue sea? Illusions.

From today on, everything is yesterday.

Of the things I think about, imprisoned in the stone of paralysis, something pleases me, and I go over it again and again: tablecloths and cheap wine in certain restaurants. Some friends drink and cut cheese while waiting for their meal. They are hardly even my colleagues. A poet, a professor, not even that.

One, triumphant, carries my lost laurel in his pocket. My name comes up and someone gives the news. Terror brushes its wing against them, first in the form of disbelief, then mocking. A laugh, eyes wide open. (What awaits me? each one thinks.) Someone asks if it's necessary to visit. No, they decide. No.

An imperfect form that desired to be perfect, an unhappy man who desired to be happy, soon I will erase myself.

I say: While in cities there remain tables with wine and tablecloths, and someone can make jokes about the breath of horror, I will be happy with the world. With this world, which I came to know despite myself.

AGNUS DEI

I, SISTER CATALINA, had to open the door to the sheep girl they brought her from the south. Pity struck me dumb.

They entrusted her to me. I rubbed her knees with oil – she couldn't walk on her feet – to get her used to my smell. Usually I sing to the children of the asylum, but she didn't understand any of the songs.

I tried to imagine her previous years as if they'd been mine. Open sky, land, fleece appeared in my memory. I cut the mass of caltrop that was her hair.

The other children looked up at my window when they went to play in the patio.

I slept with her, since she suffered. One room, one bed. They meant nothing to her.

Perhaps some had warned her: one night the Mother Superior caught me bleating.

'I gave her to you to make her human,' she said. 'And you're turning into a sheep?'

Oh yes, I wanted to say, but not fast enough.

I got in the habit of praying, 'Lamb of God, have mercy.'

Mercy he did have. She never smiled. My triumph – a sad one – were her tears; once.

Then she died.

It was in September 1911.

Now I am blind, disabled, nearly a century old. Dozens of creatures inhabit my thoughts. For me, they have never grown up. They accompany me and I accompany them in a suspended time. When the Lord calls me I will carry them with me. I only await one thing: her greeting. At the holy gates, I hope to see her smile, which I attempted to draw out uselessly. Her farewell before she died was a bleat.

GARDEN OF THE MERCIES

Through me one can travel towards every place, towards no place.

I am a garden, a park, paths running between grasses, a wall.

Walkers move through me towards no place, towards every place. One of them has encamped beneath a tree; another one, in the silence.

Here blows the wind of never, of never ever. In it swirl petals from flowers that perhaps were splendorous. But weak, like frost flowers on panes. A breath of the world erased them. Rose-coloured, leaf-ribs of blue mist destined for a processional carpet.

If here remains any ear prone to music, close it down; certain noises abide.

If any eye still likes to see, wrap it in the gauze of night.

The air enclosed in me is like no other air. It has a name, but to keep it concealed let's call it Calvary.

Through me one can travel... some might know where, and will say it in due time.

Garden, they call me, hospice of the Mercies.

Mercies it has not been my fortune to know.

A LONER

For H.A.M.

T HE LIFE OF A LONER is just that: the life of a loner. No one scattered in the multiple existence of family life can imagine the way certain perceptions of the recluse set about crystallising. The slowness of the current of habit, the fluctuation like that of a flag in the sleepy air of the tropics, the move from habit to obsession, obsession to habit. The attention to detail. A life marked by signs, milestones, omens.

That is to say, a liturgy. A liturgy that condenses and expresses something, but what? Perhaps only the adaptation through the years of a particular being to the ever growing enigma of existence. A being who can only live alone, and who becomes ever less comprehensible to himself, yet more comfortable. Comfortable in a limited sense. The survivor of a shipwreck who has got used to the plank holding him, splintered but even so offering a minimum of hospitality, or at least some inclination to mutual interaction.

A loner.

This is how things happened.

Don Pino said he would sell his restaurant.

Of all his clients, only the loners took the news as if they'd just heard a rumble of thunder. There are accurate forecasters, such as snakes and toads. Also others less precise, like, say, a sudden pain in the feet. Some are indifferent to these signs, or mistaken in their readings. But loners know.

Don Pino's announcement reverberated in their imaginations with an echoing roar.

What loners? Strictly speaking, there were three.

In the eating section, Teresina, the principal of a school, and Alberto Frin, a poet.

Both usually arrived just before noon. In the empty restaurant, their tables were just two cells, two monosyllables solved in a crossword just started.

The third loner was Emilio, Don Emilio. He sat at a desk overlooking the tables; he kept the accounts. When waiters delivered orders and loaded trays, he wrote down what was on them, he charged and gave change. He had another occupation, the one that really mattered to him, one may presume. Music. He made all his albums available to Don Pino, or rather to Don Pino's restaurant, music that had something old-fashioned about it, tangos and boleros. They made the place pleasant for diners, who were rarely young. He even had rare and coveted albums, as more than one had confirmed by approaching the desk and asking their price. Useless attempts, since he wouldn't sell for anything.

Emilio made himself as available to the restaurant as his record library. He had worked for free for thirty years. He had a head of yellowish hair. His was a passive, patient, lunar nature. A lonely one too.

How was the thunder heard by the loners at the tables? Teresina, who had the soft appearance of an archangel or someone behind thick blurred glass, reacted with melancholy. Alberto felt deep distress. *Take this chalice from me.*

It sounded otherwise to Emilio. He must have known the news already, although no one ever saw him talking to the boss. But is speech necessary, anyhow? The slow boil of a decision is enough, one that lets out bubbles at intervals, a word today and another tomorrow. Or not even a word. A curse at a new display of the son's imbecility, or silence. Emilio had sensed the change for a long time already, yes. Don Emilio did not let himself cry. He died the spring after the change of ownership, his records carefully stacked beside his bed.

Neither Don Pino nor his son attended the funeral, but a few waiters did. Let's move on from that event.

For the waiters, the news also echoed like a thunderbolt. Thirty years treading the same paths, delivering and taking away full and empty plates, listening to opinions and secretly getting tipsy on Don Pino's red wine mean something. It means something to enter a restaurant at twenty years old and hear thunder at fifty. They reacted in different ways. One spirit was broken forever. Another retired. Almost all managed somehow.

In a hermit's day, no milestone is meaningless, just as for a seagull the crags of each sunset are ballast that give stability to each day. For Alberto Frin, the food at Pino's was an important landmark. It was the same for Teresina. She had her school, with its students and parents. But that was rather a loose net, woven, so to say, on just one side of life. The waiters at Pino's had a similar role, wove a similar net in the life of Frin.

He left his house at 11.45, almost always trembling with cold. He bought cigarettes halfway down the block, and continued to the restaurant. Buying cigarettes was the first landmark. If one morning the brand he smoked wasn't there, he felt a certain distress, hard to accept as chance. Even the neighbours he met or didn't meet in the elevator held some meaning.

These facts, which a member of a family usually absorbs without a second thought, mark the hours of certain sensitive loners. They are like words printed in capital letters.

The waiters at Pino's with their white jackets and their idiosyncrasies were essential for Frin, and had been so throughout the years. A source of education. A balm. The sarcastic tenderness, the true friendship disguised as jokes had led that too lonely young man to confidence in humankind in one of its forms. He almost even reached that abandonment or at least that capacity for rest only achieved by love.

Love, no less, that milk of the soul, they had given and still gave. Those men had been the nursemaids of an always excessive, violently concealed thirst. They had been the secret source, one that flowed through hidden waterways, of a spiritual appeasement.

When the passage of the years brought to Frin's attention, in the way a step was taken or a tray carried, the mortal condition whose discovery burns with the caustic of compassion those of an imaginative nature, the waiters knew how to defend themselves. They raised the shield of humour.

Humour, the incarnation of human immortality, rose up to reject the fluid of compassion, which, anyway, was never openly displayed. Or rather, to assimilate it in a certain way beneficial to both sides. It excluded the blasphemy of sentimentalism. But there is no friendship without compassion. They, the pitied ones, felt compassion for this too proud and susceptible young man, who just like them had arrived at his fifties. Yes, they were friends.

Thus was the cloth of love woven. Nothing more and nothing less. Every lunch, every noon. As befits men, there were no questions asked, no confidences. A long absence, the publication of a book announced in a newspaper, never drifted into overly personal subjects, as it does as soon as women speak. Delicacy, which like modesty is more genuine and exquisite in men, was exercised with the greatest care. Don Emilio's music might be a little heavy, a red-hot iron in the ear of a nervous patron, but Frin wouldn't complain. An opinion of his on the restaurant menu might be a little repetitive, but the waiters would receive as if it were new.

Then that thunder sounded. Don Pino was selling. And he sold.

Now I would like you to imagine water in movement, the murky mirror filled with whirlpools usually almost imperceptible, which is life. How would this water, apparently unmoving but secretly living, appear to a group of agitated tourists with beach umbrellas, Thermoses and bathing suits? How does this group see? What does it see in the water? A fisherman, eye on the line, sitting in silence, as the dew on the shore gives way to the sun and the shadows cross from one side of a trunk to the other before the stars emerge, is able to notice changes in the current's tone. Any palpitation in the fluidity, false transparency, movement around a piece of timber or splash would hold meaning for him. Not just for him. They exist in themselves. And they cannot be seen by tourists.

For Frin this ripple was Don Pino's announcement: an appearance filled with news. News which concerned him.

The news came after the sale itself.

There wasn't a huge amount of it. News is supposed to arrive with no warning. It has a hidden side which we don't even call news, although that's what it is.

Pino's restaurant never even closed. One afternoon the tables and chairs were swapped out for more expensive ones. Prices shot up, and the food decayed to the point of tasting like gruel, the soft runny mash of those days that lacked salt and had an aftertaste of dishwater. Some screens that had given privacy were removed. The music was changed, no longer Emilio's nostalgic tracks, and the homemade pastas disappeared. The restaurant had a new name, and remained almost empty for a longish time, months. An expanse of white tablecloths which looked a bit like photographs of Antarctica at sunset with sky-blue shadows. Teresina continued to go there before noon, but Alberto Frin tried to manage otherwise. He began to cook at home.

There's no need to dwell on the cooking of a man who's never cooked. Sometimes he preferred to go without eating, but he made progress. He developed an interest in cooking. Every now and then he lost heart and resorted to sandwiches, beer. But the fatigue of poor nutrition forced him to change his ways, and he would return to the restaurant for a week or so, until the prices and repulsion forced him out again. And then he would try once more to cook.

A slow current of water in a secret whirlpool.

Men need other human beings. Even loners do. Saint Anthony crawled wearily out of the rocky den where his temptations and his ecstasies took place; he made his way to a convent near the Red Sea where pilgrims awaited. Soon, he headed back to his cave.

Alberto Frin did not have a job. A hermit's scarce need for the companionship of others is often polished off by the hard edges of a working life. At the end of the day, he seeks retreat once again with voluptuousness. Thus it was with Teresina and her school. Ever since he was young, Frin had invested all the effort many use to get a good job into the opposite, avoiding one. He didn't live on air; he proofread, translated and wrote book reviews. But he did all of this from home.

When young, he had sold lottery tickets on the boardwalk of a seaside resort. Then he was an usher at a neighbourhood movie theatre, excellent work by his standards, but he had to leave after a too violent romance with the daughter of the owner. At fifty years old he was translating articles from German for a medical magazine, and novels from English and French for a publishing house.

His poems appeared in European newspapers, as well as in Latin American magazines, always accompanied by unjustly truculent illustrations. After looking at them for a moment in such a guise, he threw them in the basket, and the woman who came to clean once a week used them along with the other old newspapers to line the garbage can.

Frin's peers had been the waiters at Pino's restaurant. Women were another story; sex has little relationship with fellow feeling. Love... Considerable damages at his apartment bore witness to fits of desperation following a love that ended. But that had been years ago.

Forced from the restaurant out of disgust for its dishes, fury at the prices and the impossibility of speaking with the old waiters due to the loudness of the music, Frin drifted aimlessly along another path.

The relationship of a loner with the drinking establishments surrounding his home is complex. Some simple souls prefer to become customers of the nearest bar. Frin was not a simple soul, but he was an extraordinary walker. When he walked, his ideas got moving like coal-driven locomotives, throwing out sparks and puffs of smoke, poems swirling into form inside his head. He burst into bars like someone walking in the clouds who's decided the fate of a storm kicking at rays of lightning and thunder bolts. He felt winged, in a state of illumination. The barmen hurried to serve him when they saw him. Those in the nearest bars to the south, north and east (to the west there was only Pino's restaurant) already knew what whisky he liked. Everyone appreciated him and served him in excess, since his payment was always exaggerated, even in periods when he dined on cheese and bread; at such times, he'd drink Hollands instead of whisky. He let a few bills drop on the counter as if he had forgotten them, no grand gesture.

Yes, he was familiar to the barmen as well as the other clients. The latter appreciated him because bar patrons are loners. To make the acquaintance of the loneliest of all, gifted with winged feet that made him even more ungraspable, pleased them. He never suspected his popularity. He believed that he was invisible, or in the case of those he knew, hated. An error, based on the legions of enemies who panted hostilities at him from the shadows of the literary reviews. But the corridors of a speciality are one thing, the wide world another.

At fifty, Alberto Frin entered what some call the dark night of the soul. It coincided with the sale of the restaurant. Don Pino, for one, would have found it perfectly natural for this crisis to be solely explained on the grounds of his retirement from the gastronomic union. But life is more complicated.

Frin's health also suffered in those days, and he had to leave off his walks. Guided by small flurries in the water just as the cork of a fisherman bobs along after being let go, carried to other temperatures and velocities and suffering transformations in his being, Alberto Frin was carried through melancholy and physical fatigue and the closing down of Pino's restaurant to seek spiritual sustenance at Moreiro's bar.

It wasn't that it was unknown to him. But the shadow of the dark night, when neither poems nor thoughts appeared to accompany him, incapable of the old walks that had carried him flying along the city's broken and filthy pavements, led him to a temporary rest at the old watering hole. The circles of life made a soothing hollow around him. Alberto Frin found himself asking Moreiro, the biggest, most intelligent, most sardonic of the blond Spaniards who had arrived there in 1950, how his family prepared stew.

When one resorts to talking about things like this, the nursemaids of the soul go back to work.

Moreiro's conversation with Alberto Frin was interesting for them both. His stop at the counter allowed for the resurfacing of muted sympathies raised by twenty years of appearances and disappearances. The man who renounces movement will see the world move. Even the hermit in the forest will watch the plants grow, and the most reclusive animals will stretch themselves out by his legs.

Sitting at Moreiro's counter, Frin heard a shy joke from a nearby table about the stew. It came from a skinny sixty-something, hunched over and frizzy-headed. Matías. An electrician, he told people, although his excuses for not showing up were known far better than any job he'd done. He spoke Spanish with a heavy accent, less German than Yiddish.

Alberto Frin knew him by sight. Living on a street for twenty years means something. Many conscious or unconscious connections are formed.

The conversation became a triangle, two at the counter and one at the table. And Frin's soul discovered his fellow men's thoughts.

One must imagine a gardener who, on the way to the palace where he works, sits down to rest in a vacant lot. There he discovers the beauty of the weeds that surround him, the grace of their leaves and their grains moved by wind. So the soul of Frin was enchanted. The shuddering spirit that only drank the wine of the gods encountered in the water of each day an immortal wine.

Pino's waiters had been something else. Those nurse-maids of the soul had spoken and laughed as they served meals, but the crowd at Moreiro's bar had no relationship with food. A coffee or a few drinks were enough excuse to stay a while in those peaceful waters, under the neon lights, reading an evening newspaper or chatting with a neighbour at the table. In the light and shadows, their souls floated and expanded like algae before flowing back to their owners at the hour for sleep, nourished by those oblique exchanges with humankind.

A club of loners, that's what the bar was.

Moreiro and his brothers, who were vigorous and married and fathers to thriving children elsewhere, gathered there to feed the lonely ones. As if from inside an aquarium, they watched the newspaper seller, a creature somewhat similar to the bar's clientele, though endowed with cirrhosis and a murder in his past; he and his wares were adhered to the glass from the outside.

Not all was silence. There were yells during games of cards, domino or dice, discussions about football and shouts into the public telephone. But not at night. And all the sounds floated above the essential damper of silence in a bar, a silence that was wholesome for them all.

On those quiet nights, Frin and Matías exchanged sarcastic remarks about German pronunciation and commentaries on the effects of race on man, a theme that interested them all. The strangeness of the Celtic spirit, and its differences with respect to the Latin, Germanic

and Judaic, were taken up with jokes and brief definitions. Scepticism about politics and a certain primordial
anarchism characterised all those men.

One day Diogenes joined their group.

Twenty years before, during a period when cigarettes
were scarce, Alberto Frin had offered a packet to Diogenes
in that bar. Since then Diogenes had considered him a
friend, although they crossed paths without greeting. Now
he made a joke from the counter, and was incorporated
into the dialogue.

Discreet and delicate just as the talks at the restaurant, but with the added nuance of the later hour, the
dialogues ranged over any theme that occurred to them.
They also avoided others, although not intentionally.
The celebration of a winning racehorse years before or
a commentary on a beautiful woman might come up, but
this was the exception. Topics expressing the most intense
ordinariness of being, such as the increases in prices, were
treated with the grace of exceptional spirits. For that is
what these men were.

Chance had played no role in their gathering. The
decanting process of life isolates the best of some human
compounds over the years, in a kind of suspension in
which a tincture of subtle elements is achieved. Whatever
it is that saturates the streets of old cities with culture can
also tint the substrate of souls. This compound loosens

during a meeting of inveterate or chance loners, such as in a bar at night. Culture is the most appropriate word for it. When a bar possesses, besides the daily debris that the flow of life accumulates on its tables, that condensation, made up of two or three patrons duly provided with the just degree of renunciation, acceptance of fate and rebellion against vulgarity, which is often the result of holding on to a hermit's vocation for many decades, the publican can be assured that a flickering light, the reddish, perplexed light of spirit, rises at night between the gloomy walls of his establishment, under the neon lighting.

With some hermits in bars there are other underlying layers, such as meanness, envy and insults. But that was not the case here.

Diogenes earned his living by drawing clock faces; his designs were highly polished. One afternoon he showed them to Frin, thereby earning his unconditional admiration. Diogenes was gentle, pink and somewhat bald, a native of Madrid who had arrived as a child with his struggling parents. There was one point he himself couldn't understand: his success in love. He took advantage of it without reflecting on it too much. Frin saw astrological reasons for it. Diogenes smiled, interested.

One hour of conversation or maybe two. With Moreiro, his brothers, Matías and Diogenes, partial combinations or all at the same time. Afterwards Frin left the bar to go home. A newt that has received its quota of air on a rock and dives into the salty green will feel a shiver of pleasure, swimming with free movements in the cold currents, at the unimaginable depths where he has chosen to live. He left the illuminated zone behind and entered his solitude, made echoless by the dark night.

Dark night. A phrase that poorly describes a state that doesn't even have the quality of night. Nothing lurks there, no light, no terror. A landscape without echoes, a kind of deprivation of the senses in which ears, palate, eyes, fingers and nose give no help. There are no signs. A corridor which isn't even a corridor, devoid of walls and apparently leading nowhere. It's not even dark, but merely opaque. The only path is to go on. But where?

There he was.

There are different kinds of people. Diggers, climbers, dreamers. Alberto Frin was the taut string of a trembling instrument. Related sounds triggered in him sympathetic vibrations, always excessive. A spiritual revelation could make him cry, alone, leaning on his worn door, from emotion, gratitude, admiration. Lightning bolts of the eternal expressed by a remote Arab, a piece of music, a paragraph in the newspaper or the expression of a profile glimpsed in the street constituted a very precise alphabet with an intensity that consumed him. His poems expressed no naive intuitions nor were they aesthetic paths. They referred to experiences of a reality hidden behind the visible; mystical, if one must give them a name. They contained mysterious references not understood by everyone. In that world of strange and supernatural sounds, afternoons of angst left him prostrate, and joys transfigured him. And periods when he felt crushed, irritable and furious and made him enigmatic.

Nothing he could share. What could he explicitly tell the waiters at Pino's, the fellow customers at Moreiro's or the enthusiastic women who came into his bed and whom he saw off afterwards without much conversation? Tacit exchanges were hidden behind common acts.

In the narrow world of local literature, his appearances produced unease and rage against what seemed untoward and misplaced. He lacked the gift of small talk. It would have seemed natural to see him open a window and leave, walking away on the air with his absorbed, magnetic and vulnerable look. Reduced to the ordinary life of ordinary mortals, like an insect with burnt antennae, he kept going to Moreiro's bar.

A stream. It sparkles on stones, resounds. A feature of the landscape brings it to a sudden halt. We see the litheness of the shimmering element, its wavelets pregnant with oxygen, flatten into a circular pool. Pool. It seems murky compared to the current that feeds it, that is itself. No observer can easily recognise the icy essence of mountain ranges in its transformation. What is free and pure takes on a murkiness that seems to stem from other lives, related to decomposition. Greenness begins to show in this environment devoid of the oxygen-delirium it carried on its way there.

The water does not know what's happening. It feels death within itself. Pullulating breeding takes advantage of the absence of the cold and pressure to set in, and the trapped water, halted and murky, accepts it. A film of unhappiness stretches over it, but it does not protest. Feeling death, it resigns itself to the absence of movement, the absence of wind, the absence of intoxication. It splashes softly against the edges and no one notes its suffering, its confusion.

This is how Alberto Frin splashed against the shores, stones and plants which were Moreiro's bar. In the times when he was a running stream, they had seen him entering, drinking and leaving, his facial features transfigured, his eyes bright as crystal, his step belonging to the air more than the pavement. Now, they felt the softness of his gentle splashing as he came to stay and talk about politics, chance, episodes of the Second World War.

Once he recognised that Diogenes was also a loner, he told him of the existence of the chicory salad, which he considered one of the great discoveries of his time in the kitchen. He was surprised when he found that not only did Diogenes know about chicory, but he held it in contempt with all his soul. Frin's hermit totalitarianism allowed for the possibility of discrepancy. He laughed. It was as if a coin had fallen in the piggy bank of his faith in humanity.

When he left, his loneliness waited for him just as a car might for others: private, no longer splendid.

He did not complain. But he felt his being was nothing more than one big question. He felt wonder at the silence of the universe, and felt his death in that silence. Insomnia, sadness, fatigue and, besides, a muting of the world. Humiliation, it might be said. The gods no longer let fall their feathers, poems, when they flew over him. He accepted this without drama. But he felt as if he was carrying an enormous burden.

The other men at the bar noticed that the slenderness that had made him seem a stranger was changing to fuller lines. Without comment (men don't get bogged down in the dirt that interests women) they admitted this as a sign of his likening to themselves, a mixing with their essences. This was an error too, and they knew it. The spring of a step, the tone of a reply, the illumination of his face showed them clearly at times that someone very different accompanied them. A group of country horses tied alongside a purebred racehorse notices without too much effort that they are not equal. Frin was a teaching or a warning for them. About what? About the mystery of the world, one might say. Yes, about the mystery of the world.

Frin was a jewel, an honour and a gift. Not in an explicit way. But his ironies, striking definitions, and arbitrary and surprising judgements were like the diving of a marine bird that disappears from the world of reason and re-emerges with prey in its beak. It was invigorating for them. They did not suspect Frin's sadness, his distress. He amazed them with his ability to laugh at another man's wit, a display of innocence. They admired him without realising it, in a simple and everyday way. They were friends.

It was a calm night.

Matías had just understood a truth. Taking a break from the copy of *Frankfurter Allgemeine* – a paper that Frin subscribed to and passed on to him – now folded next to his cup of coffee, he'd heard Diogenes crack a joke about his personality. It concerned a certain burnt-out light in Diogenes' house. Matías had maintained through an entire year that it was a special case. In other words, he had no intention of fixing it.

Frin, who had drunk a lot, looked at him in the strangest way and asked him a question. Through that question Matías understood the principle that constituted his root. To put it another way, he understood himself. He saw that the idleness he defended at the heart of poverty and the isolation he treasured were what made life livable. That was the very essence of himself. If he were to fix Diogenes' light, he would begin to fix others' as well, and that would be the death of him. He would die just as Don Emilio had died, when he hadn't been able to play music on his albums or pass the time with addition and subtraction. He would die from suffocation, the absence of a vital element. Teresina would probably have died too, or lost her archangelic features, had she carried on the presumed obligation of living with her aged parents.

Matías understood himself. He saw clearly who he was. He found peace.

It was a quiet night. Moreiro the younger passed a cloth over the counter. A gentle young man, the father of three boys, he had been in jail for a year. Revenge of the police, whom he had charged for what they had drunk out of inexperience. 'If there is a God,' he said, 'someone will pay. If there is not, patience.' A year in the filth of the jail and he emerged as tender and merciful as he had entered.

Then, in that stillness amidst the dialogue, a noise started. A din that filled the room from floor to ceiling, making it impossible to hear anything else. The sound of a shouting man. He was yelling at Moreiro the younger. The man was huge. He leaned on the bar.

Frin swivelled round to look at him. He took Moreiro's metal tray and slammed it on his table with a crashing Doomsday sound. The man turned.

He looked at the three customers, who didn't look at him. Diogenes was pink-faced, Frin's hair stuck out as if blown in a stiff wind, Matías leaned with his nose over the coffee.

'I know who did that...' the man murmured, moving forward.

He held out his arms for balance, opened and closed his hands.

Something happened.

Diogenes stood up, taking his chair along with him, and walked to the man. His slightly bald, tame head leaned over the raised chair. He clapped the legs of the chair against the man and used it to push him back. Something about him reminded you of those wasps that can drag a spider three times their size.

He pushed him all the way to the pavement and then punched his face. Blood began to fall. Frin jumped out to the pavement and cleaned the blood from the man with his handkerchief, murmuring 'There, there,' like the tamer of a bear with a crushed paw.

Then another man appeared, moving between the tables. He had a thin beard and a garland of rags tied to his hat. Stretching out his arms, he yelled, 'Long live the nation!'

He turned and left. At the door he made an obscene noise.

'Long live the nation!' he shouted again, and disappeared.

A long round of laughter began. Moreiro the elder started, his blue eyes sparkling, and Diogenes followed, then Frin, leaning on the door with his back. Matías laughed, his chin shaking. Moreiro the younger laughed, wet with tears he'd never shown. The man who had yelled, his lapel streaming with blood, laughed with immense guffaws.

Laughter woke up the windows, display cases and mirror, sweeping clean the entire bar and the souls of those in it.

Then there was silence. Moreiro the elder uncorked a bottle of Spanish brandy.

'On the house.'

The younger brother lined up six new glasses, and they all drank, savouring, breathing in.

At half past three Frin got up. 'See you tomorrow,' he said.

On the pavement he found the air of the night. Also, the beginning of a poem.

Resigned to the wasteland, he didn't recognise it. He didn't recognise it in the phrase that first suggested itself, then returned, a feather from the wing of the gods.

He picked it up.

Something was beginning.

Pushkin Press

Pushkin Press was founded in 1997, and publishes novels, essays, memoirs, children's books—everything from timeless classics to the urgent and contemporary.

This book is part of the Pushkin Collection of paperbacks, designed to be as satisfying as possible to hold and to enjoy. It is typeset in Monotype Baskerville, based on the transitional English serif typeface designed in the mid-eighteenth century by John Baskerville. It was litho-printed on Munken Premium White Paper and notch-bound by the independently owned printer TJ International in Padstow, Cornwall. The cover, with French flaps, was printed on Rives Linear Bright White paper. The paper and cover board are both acid-free and Forest Stewardship Council (FSC) certified.

Pushkin Press publishes the best writing from around the world—great stories, beautifully produced, to be read and read again.

STEFAN ZWEIG · EDGAR ALLAN POE · ISAAC BABEL
TOMÁS GONZÁLEZ · ULRICH PLENZDORF · JOSEPH KESSEL
VELIBOR ČOLIĆ · LOUISE DE VILMORIN · MARCEL AYMÉ
ALEXANDER PUSHKIN · MAXIM BILLER · JULIEN GRACQ
BROTHERS GRIMM · HUGO VON HOFMANNSTHAL
GEORGE SAND · PHILIPPE BEAUSSANT · IVÁN REPILA
E.T.A. HOFFMANN · ALEXANDER LERNET-HOLENIA
YASUSHI INOUE · HENRY JAMES · FRIEDRICH TORBERG
ARTHUR SCHNITZLER · ANTOINE DE SAINT-EXUPÉRY
MACHI TAWARA · GAITO GAZDANOV · HERMANN HESSE
LOUIS COUPERUS · JAN JACOB SLAUERHOFF
PAUL MORAND · MARK TWAIN · PAUL FOURNEL
ANTAL SZERB · JONA OBERSKI · MEDARDO FRAILE
HÉCTOR ABAD · PETER HANDKE · ERNST WEISS
PENELOPE DELTA · RAYMOND RADIGUET · PETR KRÁL
ITALO SVEVO · RÉGIS DEBRAY · BRUNO SCHULZ · TEFFI
EGON HOSTOVSKÝ · JOHANNES URZIDIL · JÓZEF WITTLIN